DEPTH CHARGE

A NOVEL BY JASON HEATON

swimpruf
PRESS

This is a work of fiction. Names, characters, businesses, places, events, locales, and incidents are either the products of the author's imagination or used in a fictitious manner. Any resemblance to actual persons, living or dead, or actual events is purely coincidental.

Published by Swimpruf Press, Minneapolis
www.swimpruf.com

First Edition, April, 2021

Cover design, map, and diagram by Paul Andrews.

DEPTH
CHARGE

+

INDIA

SRI
LANKA

Trincomalee

Pasikudah

Batticaloa

Kandy

Colombo

Pottuvil

Galle

Indian Ocean

DIVE SUPPORT VESSEL DEPTH CHARGE

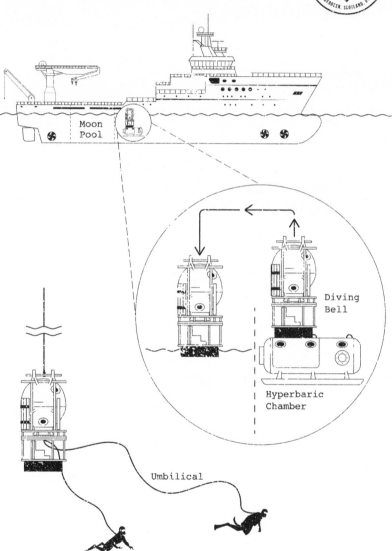

Moon
Pool

Diving
Bell

Hyperbaric
Chamber

Umbilical

Contents

CONTENTS

DEPTH CHARGE

For Gishani, and for Mom, my two Number One fans

DEPTH CHARGE

"You don't reach Serendib by plotting a course for it. You have to set out in good faith for elsewhere and lose your bearings."

— John Barth, *The Last Voyage of Somebody the Sailor*

DEPTH CHARGE

Prologue

Cavendish Laboratories, Cambridge, England.
9 April, 1942

"Sir John, there's someone here to see you." Sir John Havelock's secretary averted eye contact, knowing her boss hated to be disturbed. "He says it's urgent," she added, to emphasize that this interruption was not her idea.

"Send him in, Mary," Havelock grumbled without looking up from his desk. His consent mattered little, as the man strode into the office before the secretary had turned to go. Havelock glanced up and then did a double take. The man was young, but with a maturity on his face that war lends. He was dressed in the dark blue wool of a Royal Navy greatcoat, its gilt buttons glittering in the faint light of the dim office.

"Lieutenant James McGuinn, Sir John," he said in a hurried voice with a hint of an Irish accent. "I'm afraid I have some bad news." It could only be bad when a naval officer made the trip to Cambridge. This week of all weeks, Havelock feared the worst.

"We've lost HMAS *Vampire*, sir," McGuinn said, his

1

voice breaking. Havelock slowly set down his pen and swiveled his leather chair to face the windows. Dusty shafts of light angled through the scrim-taped X's. "Japs sunk her and *Hermes* off of Ceylon. Only nine lost, but *Hermes* lost over 300 at last count."

Havelock didn't care about the crew at the moment. He could only think of *Vampire*'s precious cargo, now lying on the bottom of the Indian Ocean. He needed to know if it was safe. This was a question he couldn't ask the young lieutenant who stood across his desk, now uncomfortably clearing his throat. There were only a handful who knew what the destroyer was carrying.

"And... Commander Moran?" Havelock tried to sound casual but concerned. Moran was one of the handful. After all, *Vampire* was his ship.

"I'm afraid he went down with her, according to survivors' accounts," McGuinn replied, finding it curious that Havelock would inquire only after the captain. Perhaps they were friends.

In fact, Sir John Havelock had never met Commander William Thomas Alldis Moran, Royal Australian Navy. Havelock was a civilian, a scientist who hadn't left England since the war began, but he'd learned enough about Moran to trust him with England's top secret. Born in Fremantle, Moran had served as a torpedo man in the British Royal Navy before being promoted to Commander at the relatively young age of 33. By 1940, he was given command of Australia's HMAS *Vampire*, a scrappy 300-foot destroyer that saw plenty of action, including surviving the fierce bombardment off of Malaya that sunk two battleships, HMS *Repulse* and *Prince of Wales.*

"Will there be anything else, sir?"

The question stirred Havelock from his thoughts. "No, thank you, Lieutenant," he said with a somber smile and stood to shake the man's hand. "A pity about this loss. One day we'll avenge their deaths."

An oddly belligerent remark from this tweedy scientist, thought McGuinn as he turned to leave the office, wondering why he was told to deliver the news of a specific naval loss to an academic in Cambridge.

Once he was gone, Havelock pushed back his chair with a defiant huff and walked to the door, calling out to his secretary, "Mary, tea please. And get Paget Thomson on the phone. I need to speak with him right away."

He strode over to the windows and peered out. His office at the Cavendish Laboratories overlooked Free School Lane. It was a sunny spring morning, and the narrow street would normally have been full of students out enjoying some of the season's first warmth. Today it was nearly empty. The war seemed to have put every aspect of life on hold. Havelock turned back to his desk and wondered to himself how deep *Vampire* was. Could her cargo be salvaged? It would be risky, yes, but this was war. Risks must be taken. Mary entered his office balancing a cup and saucer.

"Everything OK, sir?" she gently asked, setting the tea down on top of some papers, along with a small pile of shortbread biscuits. "I heard that officer mention a shipwreck."

"An Australian destroyer was sunk in Ceylon," he muttered distractedly. "A shame, a great shame."

"Sorry to hear that, sir," Mary said, and turned to leave the office. "Oh, Mr. Paget Thomson will be calling shortly. He was in a meeting in London."

"Thank you, Mary." Havelock waved her off as he put his lips to the steaming cup, then pulled back. "And one more thing. I'll be needing a nautical chart of the east coast of Ceylon."

Blow Down

Bay of Bengal, eight nautical miles east of Batticaloa, Sri Lanka. Present day.

Malcolm Rausing gazed out the pilothouse window of the dive support vessel *Depth Charge* into the black night. In the distance to the west he could just make out the twinkling lights of Batticaloa. Otherwise it was pitch black, and he could hear the waves gently lapping at the hull 40 feet below. It was a new moon, so no silver beams of light on the sea, no reflection of any kind. Rausing's face was illuminated by the green light of the instrument panel in front of him. The crescent scar on his forehead stood out in relief, disappearing into his V-shaped hairline. In the artificial light, his pale blond hair, pulled back into a tight ponytail, had the cast of silver mercury. His large grey eyes were intelligent and probing as he scanned the horizon, like a nocturnal predator searching for prey. Satisfied with what he saw, he turned to face the group of three men who stood a respectful distance behind him, all of them wearing black starched shirts with epaulets and the sleeves rolled up neatly, buttoned at their biceps.

"We'll dive in an hour," Rausing said to them. "Get the divers blown down to bottom pressure."

5

"Yes, sir," the big man on the end said with a Scandinavian accent. He turned on his heel and left the pilothouse through the outside door, his footfall receding as he clanged down the metal staircase. The humid sea air had briefly entered the cabin, adding some warmth to the chill of the air conditioning.

"Scholz, make sure we have a couple of Zodiacs around the perimeter of the ship keeping an eye out for fishermen," he said to the angular man with the shaved head and mustache. Scholz nodded and also left the pilothouse, this time through the rear door to the ship's interior, leaving only the captain, a bearded, portly man with a bad complexion, and Rausing.

"The scope shows no other boats in the vicinity, and the fishing fleet won't be back this way until dawn," the captain said with the heavy tongue of an Eastern European accent. He stepped forward towards the ship's controls before catching Rausing's piercing eyes and stopping short. Rausing smiled and patted Captain Balázs Kovács on the shoulder like a principal reassuring a wary schoolboy.

"I'll leave you to it then, Captain," Rausing said. "This is your ship." Kovács knew better. He may have been responsible for driving the ship and overseeing the crew's daily duties, but Rausing was really in control. The *Depth Charge* was his boat, part of the Rausing Oceanic fleet, acquired five years earlier and retrofitted to be a dive support vessel, with a hoist, pressure chamber, hyperbaric lifeboat, and moon pool. Rausing had even changed the ship's name, ordering the paint spelling out *Baltic Star* scrubbed from its hull, in defiance of superstition. In a matter of only a few months, all remnants of its former life as a gritty North Sea salvage boat were gone, replaced by the starched uniforms and gilt logo china plates of the DSV *Depth Charge*. Captain Kovács didn't complain. Life was better than ever, with a fat salary, a sparkling refurbished ship, and the tropical climate of his new temporary home, Sri Lanka.

"I'll be in my quarters until dive time. Fetch me if anything changes out there," Rausing said, gesturing towards the black sea outside, though the windows only reflected their own green lit faces. He strode to the door and was gone. Kovács exhaled, then stepped out of the port-side door onto the stairs for a cigarette. Rausing disapproved of smoking but hadn't forbidden it other than among the team of divers, but Kovács still felt sneaky every time he lit up.

On the dive deck two levels below and aft of the pilothouse, two clean-shaven, fit-looking men were contorting into heavy dive suits made of black crushed neoprene. Few words were exchanged between them and a third man, Murray, the bell man, besides affirmatives after each zipper was snugged. The divers, Rory Aitkens and Gus McElroy—both Scots—sat side by side on a bench, sweating profusely in the tropical night air. Under their neoprene they wore woolen union suits to ward off a hypothermic chill at the sea bottom.

"Transfer to the chamber for blowdown," echoed a canned voice from a speaker mounted on the wall. It was Dive Control, the command center for all diving activities on the *Depth Charge*, housed in a dark room in the ship's belly. The divers each lifted a gloved hand to the camera mounted in the corner of the room and gave the "OK" sign with index finger and thumb pressed together.

Aitkens and McElroy were saturation divers, about as far from recreational scuba divers as a kite-flying child is from a fighter pilot. Rather than swimming freely with tanks on their backs, their breathing gas, a mix of helium and oxygen, would be continually pumped down to them through a long "umbilical" system from the support ship. This umbilical also bundled communication cables and electrical power for their headlamps and camera. A hot water system circulated warm water through their suits. Though the surface temperature of the Indian Ocean was 87 degrees Fahrenheit, at 350 feet, it would be in the 60s, enough to chill a diver working for several hours.

The divers would not travel to and from the sea bottom by their own power, but rather be transported inside a diving bell, pumped up to the same pressure as the surrounding water at depth, thus staying dry inside. Once at the bottom, the divers exited the bell and swam or walked to their work sites, where they could stay for hours. To get around lengthy decompression, the men would remain under pressure inside the bell on the way back to the surface, and then be transferred to a pressurized chamber on board the *Depth Charge*, where they could either remain at "bottom pressure" or slowly decompress for hours or even days while the ship sailed off-site.

This kind of "saturation" diving has been around since

the 1960s, and helped pioneer much of the North Sea and Gulf of Mexico oil fields, as well as numerous clandestine military operations carried out during the Cold War. But this empty stretch of Indian Ocean off the east coast of Sri Lanka held no oil reserves, nor was this a military operation.

Murray, McElroy, and Aitkens ducked into the compression chamber, a schoolbus-length tube of thick steel in the hold of the ship. This would be their home between dives and during the long decompression to bring them slowly back to surface air pressure. An attendant sealed the hatch behind them and checked for leaks. Then the chamber was "blown down," slowly pressurized to ten times the air pressure at the surface. The divers inside wiggled their jaws and blew against pinched noses as the atmosphere inside pushed against their eardrums.

A face appeared in the thick, small window halfway up the side of the chamber. It was Malcolm Rausing. He pressed a button next to the window and spoke quietly into a microphone.

"Remember what I told you," he said, "eight meters forward of the starboard rudder and three meters up from the bilge keel." The divers nodded. "Needless to say, be very careful with that cutting torch." Again, nods. Rausing made eye contact with both men, but added no smile or well wishes. Then he stepped back and was gone.

"Bottom pressure reached. Transfer to the bell," the voice from Dive Control echoed in the chamber. The divers collected their helmets and tool belts and walked heavily to a ladder that accessed a hatch in the ceiling of their chamber. Murray climbed awkwardly to the top, spun open the locking wheel, and pushed the hatch open into the diving bell. The bell, which was mated to the chamber, was pressurized to the same ten atmospheres so the hatch opened easily. He ensured all valves were positioned correctly, verified that comms worked and then signaled for McElroy and Aitkens to climb up behind him.

With the divers locked inside, the closet-sized bell was detached from the chamber and swung by a crane until it hung half submerged in the ship's moon pool, an opening to the sea in the middle of the aft deck of the *Depth Charge*. As they settled into position for their elevator ride to the bottom, the divers could see some of the crew through a thick Perspex window. They were gathered on the aft deck of the ship silhouetted against the floodlights. Rausing, the tallest, stood with arms folded, a breeze lifting his hair so it wreathed his head in a sort of glowing crown.

Up in the pilothouse, Captain Kovács hovered over a screen with a digital outline of the *Depth Charge* on it. The ship's dynamic positioning system whirred on and off, its gimbals and GPS keeping it directly above the exact sea bed coordinates Rausing had specified. All was going to plan. With any luck, they'd be hauling the divers back up in the bell and hoisting their cargo by 0600 and be back in Batticaloa an hour later—nobody the wiser but a few fishermen who'd not thought to ask questions about this gleaming ship that had been in the harbor for the past several weeks.

The hoist whined as it lowered the diving bell through the moon pool into the water. The ship's floodlights illuminated the bell as it swung gently in the ocean swells. Small fish swarmed the scene, attracted by the light. Slowly, the bell grew smaller and then disappeared from sight, leaving only a bubbling surface. Then the floodlights went dark.

Tube Alloys

Burlington House, London.
12 April, 1942

Sir John Havelock surveyed the Royal Society's meeting room at Burlington House. It was dimly lit and reeked of tobacco smoke. The other twelve members of the MAUD Committee were puffing on pipes, cigars, or cigarettes, and Havelock instinctively filled the bowl of his own briar pipe after hanging up his raincoat. A cut-glass decanter sat on a sideboard, and the men milled around, talking in hushed tones and sipping sherry from matching glasses.

A door at the end of the room creaked open. In strode George Paget Thomson, the leader of the committee, and another man wearing a dark uniform. They made an odd pair—Thomson a bookish, slightly cross-eyed scientist, the other man a lean, serious-looking military type. The banter stopped and the committee members took seats around a large central table. Rain pattered on the window and, though it was midafternoon, the gloom made it feel like late evening.

"Gents, this is Commander Ian Colter from the Royal Navy's Intelligence division," Thomson said, without even a greeting. He gestured for Colter to sit while he himself took a chair at the head of the table. "It seems that we may have a window of time in which to mount a salvage operation on the *Vampire*. Sir John has been in touch with the Australian Navy, and from what survivors have related, the ship sank fairly quickly after being hit, with most damage amidships. That bodes well for a recovery of our cargo."

Sir John Havelock nodded from his chair halfway down the table and relit his pipe. Though he was overseeing the test phase of the Tube Alloys project, he had not been a member of the MAUD Committee as long as the others; he'd been brought in only when the prototype device was nearly completed. Havelock's reputation as a physicist and test engineer had preceded him, and he commanded respect from the men around the table.

The possible loss of their only prototype was a devastating blow to the project, and Havelock took it personally. With *Vampire* and her unique cargo lying wrecked on the sea floor, it would be months before they could attempt another test. That is, unless they could salvage the device before its metal casing and complex wiring were damaged by extended exposure to seawater.

The MAUD Committee, reputed to have been named for physicist Niels Bohr's housekeeper, had been formed in 1940 by George Paget Thomson at the government's request. It was responsible for overseeing "Tube Alloys," Britain's secret project to develop an atomic weapon. England was at the forefront of atomic research, with the discoveries of both the electron and neutron at Cavendish

Laboratory in Cambridge. It was also there that the first successful nuclear fission was carried out. When British intelligence found out that the Germans were working on an atomic weapon in March of 1940, Tube Alloys was quickly made top priority.

Development of an actual bomb had been painfully slow, with the work spread out across four universities and enriched uranium sourced in Canada. Finally, in early 1942, a prototype was ready for testing. That's where Havelock came in, based on his work at Cambridge and his experience pioneering weapons test protocols between the wars. It was his meticulous refinement of wind tunnel development that earned him a visit at Cambridge from Paget Thomson.

But an atomic weapon was something entirely different. Testing had to be not only safe, but also observable and discreet. Havelock's solution had been to propose a test detonation in a remote atoll, where the weapon's effects could be viewed from ships anchored at a distance and there would be little chance of discovery by the Germans. Thomson took it up with the Ministry of Defence, who found a reluctant but ultimately willing partner in the Royal Australian Navy. The site would be the uninhabited Monte Bello island chain 120 miles north of the western Australian coast.

The prototype bomb had been loaded onto the Australian Navy destroyer HMAS *Vampire* in Gibraltar under cover of night and sailed, well escorted, around the Cape of Good Hope to avoid the U-boat infested Mediterranean. The stopover in Ceylon was supposed to be a routine refueling. Unfortunately, it had coincided with the Japanese surprise attack on Trincomalee.

HMS *Hermes*, the second ship sunk along with the *Vampire*, was the world's first purpose-built aircraft carrier, built in 1918 and would have been scrapped if not for the badly stretched Eastern fleet that made use of her flight deck to launch Fairey Swordfish biplanes. Both ships were fleeing Trincomalee harbor ahead of the Japanese attack, but were spotted and quickly pounced upon by a squadron of Mitsubishi A6M Zeros. *Hermes* took over 40 direct hits and went into a derelict circular limp before succumbing to her wounds and nosing beneath the waves, taking 309 souls with her. *Vampire* went down mercifully sooner, but with only nine crew aboard. The hospital ship, *Vita*, picked up survivors, while some managed to swim the eight miles to shore, where they were rescued by surprised villagers.

The Americans, who had suffered their own surprise attack only months earlier at Pearl Harbor, were now in the war and pressuring the British government to collaborate on an atomic "deterrent." Havelock was vehemently against the idea of sharing secrets with the Americans. He was glad they had joined the war effort, but begrudged them for taking so long while England bore the brunt of the Axis Powers' fury. He wanted Tube Alloys to remain a purely British endeavor. Call it national pride, call it official secrets—he knew once the Americans got hold of their research, Britain would be reduced to a supporting role. And with the sinking of the *Vampire*, this looked all the more inevitable.

Commander Colter stood and broke the silence in the room, his accent crisp, his tone clipped and perfunctory. "According to the last known position of *Vampire* and our own hydrographic charts, she lies in 50 to 60 fathoms." Murmurs around the table as the committee members shook their heads and looked at each other. Colter continued.

"As you surmise, gentlemen, yes, this is deep," he said. "More than twice as deep as the *Laurentic*, with which I am sure you're all familiar." There were nods around the table as he conjured the name of the famous wreck salvaged off the coast of Ireland for its government gold after the Great War. "And the southeast monsoon is still blowing in Ceylon, which will make things a bit more... sporty." Havelock thought he made this sound like an afternoon of shooting clay pigeons. "But our diving unit has the latest in underwater technology, and we have brave men who we feel can carry out this operation."

"Besides the obvious dangers of the diving," Havelock asked, "how will you be able to carry out a mission in those seas, with the Japanese Navy about?" He liked Colter's confidence but worried about yet another attack. "What if we manage to bring the bomb up, only to have it captured or destroyed by the Japanese?"

"It's a risk we're prepared to take," Colter said, as if he'd rehearsed the line, or maybe said it a dozen times in his career. "With *Hermes* sunk and Trincomalee's capabilities diminished, we've had to reroute two cruisers from the Eastern Fleet. The Australians are sending another destroyer. We assume we can load the cargo onto that

ship for further transport to your test location."
Havelock felt better knowing there would be additional
naval support. He nodded and sat back in his chair.

"We should have our diving team in place within the
week," Colter said, and sat.

"Excellent, Commander," Paget Thomson chimed in.
"We wish your men the greatest of luck." He looked
around the table. "I suggest we reconvene next week
when we've news of the operation's success." He gave
a thin smile to Colter, who didn't return it but nodded
and stood up crisply.

The committee adjourned, and a few of the men lingered,
pouring more sherry, as if toasting what they were
convinced would be a success. John Havelock wasn't
so sure. He lingered at the window, looking down at
the rain-soaked courtyard, where Commander Colter
was climbing into an Austin saloon with Royal Navy
markings. As he shut the door, the navy man glanced up,
as if sensing Havelock's gaze on him. He nodded to him
as the car drove off, joining the evening Mayfair traffic.

"Godspeed," Havelock whispered, and turned to go.
He had a train to catch back to Cambridge.

Invertebrates and a Crow's Foot

Galle, Sri Lanka.
Present day.

Julian Tusk, "Tusker" to his friends, couldn't decide
which was worse: the acrid stench of the harbor or the
detritus-strewn muddy sea floor below it. At least it was
cooler underwater. Slightly. He still wore a full-length
two-millimeter wetsuit as some protection from whatever
permeated this rainbow-sheened soup polluted with
diesel, garbage, and a city's effluence.

There were few fish—living ones, at least. The silty sea
bed was littered with the bones of discarded bycatch
and cleaned carcasses from the fishermen above, who
tossed what wasn't wanted over the side after their
night of hauling in nets offshore. Various invertebrates
occasionally scuttled across his limited field of view.
He couldn't name them. Tusker was an archaeologist,
not a biologist, and he was braving this toxic morass not
for the wildlife but rather to identify a nameless pile of
lumber unearthed in yet another of the government's
dredging projects.

The city of Galle lies on the strategic southwestern tip of
Sri Lanka. This location made it prized by the country's

European occupiers. First the Portuguese came, building a fort on a cliff high above the sea, with sweeping views from its ramparts across the Indian Ocean. Then the Dutch swept in and ruled for over a century. Finally the British added what was then called Ceylon as a coda to their East India empire. They all made use of the fort and today within its walls is a bustling town bearing the remnants of all three of its former occupiers, in varying states of charming decay: buildings with Mediterranean tiled roofs line dusty streets with Dutch names and distinctly English hotels. Galle Fort is peopled with descendants of all three occupiers, living side by side with local Sinhalese fishermen and Muslim shop owners.

Over its long history, Galle Harbor would have seen any number of its former occupiers' ships that called on the nearby fort. As he peered through the swirling cloud of silt, Tusker wondered, was this half-buried wooden spine a Portuguese barquentine? A Dutch frigate perhaps? Or just a lowly fishing boat?

Tusker's six-month stint in Sri Lanka as a visiting professor of marine archaeology meant investigating the glamorous as well as the decidedly less so. A sample of the wood poking up through the thick clay sea bed from this nameless vessel, sent to the lab in Colombo, could help pin down its age and possibly its origin. But something more substantial—a piece of china, a windlass, an anchor—would be more conclusive.

Tusker looked up from his tedious excavating. Through the haze he made out the silhouette of Upali, swimming just above the sea floor ten yards away, jabbing the sand with a long rod. Tusker nodded to him and Upali returned the gesture with a pinkie and thumb "shaka" hand signal. It was typically upbeat for Upali, who made even the most mundane work seem fun.

Upali Karuna worked for the Sri Lankan Ministry of Culture, History, and Archaeology, or "MOCHA." They'd gone to school together at Michigan Tech, just about as antipodal as you could get from the perpetually sweaty hug that was Sri Lanka. It was Upali who'd invited Tusker to Sri Lanka for a visiting fellowship, and he who had given him his nickname, a play on his last name, but also a reference to the elephants of Upali's homeland that grew big ivory. Julian latched onto it after a lifetime of hating the first name his parents had cursed him with.

After graduating, Upali had gone on to get a Ph.D. at the University of Miami and then returned to his native Sri Lanka to teach and dive, before finally settling into a director's job with MOCHA. He liked to joke that he'd invited Tusker to Sri Lanka this year as "payback" for the long winters in Michigan's Upper Peninsula and the frigid dives they'd done in the Great Lakes. "I'll keep your drysuit for you," Tusker had told him when he left. "You know you're going to miss it." That was over a decade ago and Upali had still never returned. Meanwhile, Tusker stayed on, becoming faculty at Michigan Tech, teaching underwater archaeology there, and using the plentiful shipwrecks of the Great Lakes as his classroom. As he liked to tell Upali, "It's unsalted and there are no sharks."

Tusker turned back to the task at hand. Two months

of surveying and digging had exposed a good deal of the wooden structure, but there was much to be done and work would continue long after he returned to the States. He peered at his wristwatch, a huge, old Aquastar Benthos. It was a gift from his father, who'd worn it during his stint as a support diver on the U.S. Navy's Tektite project in the early '70s. Its timing ring was faded and its case had a dent, but Tusker had faithfully kept it serviced since his father's death and it never left his wrist. He never wore a modern dive computer unless he really needed its additional functionality.

The watch's bright orange hand showed that 45 minutes had passed since their last tank swap. When he finished with this one, they'd break for lunch. Then Ian Walsh, the salty expat Brit, would swap places with Upali underwater.

Twenty minutes later, Tusker's tank was down to 200 psi. Time for lunch. He banged on his tank to get Upali's attention and gave the thumbs up "ascend" signal. Upali signaled back with an "OK" and started to ascend. Tusker slowly lifted off the sea bed, following Upali to the surface.

"'Bout time," said Ian, who was sweating profusely under his broad-brimmed hat as he leaned over the gunwale of the rickety skiff. "I'm starving."

Raj, the fisherman whose boat they'd rented for three months and who was helping them during this project, greeted Upali on the opposite side of the boat with a barrage of Sinhala and a hearty laugh.

"Got the kettle on?" Tusker smiled, handed his weight belt, tank and harness up to Ian, and heaved himself into the boat. He stripped off the upper part of his sopping wetsuit, tying the empty arms around his waist. Months in the tropics had tanned his torso a deep shade of brown, except for a long scar across his left shoulder that stood out as a slash of white. He ran a hand through his wet, sun-bleached hair, which he hadn't cut since arriving the previous autumn. Without the care of a local barber, it had grown out, saltwater and sun stiffening it to the consistency of dry grass.

In the harbor the last of the fishing fleet was tying up, a mix of rickety wooden vessels with small outboard motors, ugly fiberglass skiffs like the one they were on, and a few traditional *oruwa* catamarans. The air reeked of rotting fish and diesel exhaust. Tusker had a sudden urge to be back home. It would be spring there, woodsmoke on the wind, the smell of damp soil, still some snow in the shadows. *Heading back soon enough*, he thought, and shook off the daydream.

"Anything promising down there today?" Ian asked once they'd settled in the skiff.

"No luck today, it seems," Upali said. "Not exactly the way I wanted to finish out the week before I head over to Batticaloa."

"You sure chose a fine time to abandon us here," Tusker jabbed him, shaking his head. Upali laughed.

"Yeah, another posh holiday disguised as official business," Ian chimed in. "What is it this time? Interviewing female interns poolside?"

"All right, all right, guys," Upali shook his head. "It might be another goose chase, but a fisherman reported snagging his lines on something deep offshore. HQ figured it'd be worth looking into, given all the lost war wrecks over there. I'm going to make a search grid and run some sonar scans."

"A likely story," Tusker replied. "You get the glamorous gigs while Ian and I are left here to dig in the mud." He grinned at his friend and winked behind his sunglasses. "Batticaloa," Tusker stumbled on the town's name, "That's a fair drive to get there, yeah?"

"From here it'll be a good six hours cross-country. The funny thing is, it's only about 350 kilometers. In the U.S., that'd take you two, maybe two and a half hours? But here, it's all narrow roads and lots of small towns."

"Oh, I'm well familiar now," Tusker said. "I certainly will not miss the traffic here when I go back home. Where are you staying over there?"

"For the east coast work, MOCHA partners with a dive resort in Batti called the Deep Blue. They cater to the tech diving crowd, these macho foreigners who want to tick the *Hermes* off their bucket list," Upali said, referring to the wreck of the British aircraft carrier sunk by a Japanese aerial attack during World War II. "If I get some free time, I might do a dive or two. I need to keep my proficiency up, you know." He grinned.

"Ah, the truth comes out," Ian replied as he fished their lunch packets out of a sun-faded cooler. "A diving holiday!"

Raj's mobile phone interrupted the banter, ringing shrilly. He wiggled his head side to side in apology and fished it out of his shirt pocket. He spoke in animated Sinhala for less than a minute, then put the phone away and said something to Upali.

"That was a call from the guy who's fixing the pump," Upali translated. The tired dredging pump they'd been using to excavate sea bed had sputtered to a halt two days earlier. It required constant fiddling to keep running, but it did make their work a lot easier. They'd finally left it with a motorcycle mechanic in Galle to tinker with. "Sounds like it might be ready this afternoon."

Tusker gave an exaggerated double "thumbs up" gesture. "Well, that's some good news. Ian, if you want to go into town and pick it up, we can keep at it since we're already suited up." Tusker gestured to Upali and then at the muddy harbor. He took a pull on an insulated flask that had lost its battle with the tropical sun and got a mouthful of lukewarm water that tasted faintly of iodine.

"Right-o, I'm sure it just took a little gaffer tape and a whack with a big spanner," Ian replied in his sharp Geordie accent. "I'll go pick it up in the van and then start my weekend early." He grinned.

"Got a big date, Ian?" Upali asked. "Still pursuing that

waitress at The Lighthouse?"

"I'm waiting for you to teach me some more Sinhala so I can impress her!" Ian shot back.

"I'm not sure what would confuse her more, your Newcastle accent or your attempted Sinhala!"

Tusker laughed out loud. "Seriously, Ian. People say I sound like the characters in that show, *Fargo*, but the Midwestern U.S. has got nothing on the north of England when it comes to accents. It's taken me six months to finally understand a word you're saying."

"Oh sure, you betcha," Upali said in an exaggerated Midwestern American accent. Tusker punched him hard on the shoulder.

"Hey man, you spent enough time in Houghton to pick it up. Now you've got a weird mish-mash of Sri Lankan and Yooper," Tusker joked, referring to the nickname given to Michigan's Upper Peninsula natives.

After a short lunch of red rice and jackfruit curry eaten out of a banana leaf on the sweltering skiff, Tusker wriggled back into his damp wetsuit and spat in his mask. Raj would take Ian back to the dock while Upali and Tusker were underwater, returning with the skiff. They bade farewell to Ian, heaved their air cylinders onto their backs and backrolled off opposite gunwales. The commotion scattered a group of gulls floating nearby. As soon as they reached the bottom, Tusker heard the outboard motor start up and watched the silhouette of the boat swing around and disappear.

Upali and Tusker spread out, picking around the search area they'd marked with yellow flags, probing the deep silt with wire probes, stopping to mark promising spots with red flags.

Next week, best bring the metal detector and some hand tools to investigate all these. Tusker mentally prepped for next week to fill the monotony. *Wouldn't Upali be jealous if I find something while he's over on the east coast.* He smiled to himself.

At four o'clock, after two more tank swaps, they were ready to call it a day. The sun dropped like a stone in the tropics, meaning it would be dark in two hours. Underwater, it was already getting hard to see in the late afternoon light. Probing, flagging, and digging was monotonous, exhausting work, especially while sucking dry, compressed air. Despite the bathtub-warm water, Tusker was thoroughly chilled.

Raj, whose day sitting in the skiff under the hot sun had been no less arduous, helped them heave their gear into the boat. They motored across the crowded harbor to a dock. Tusker tugged on the faded red Mount Gay Rum baseball cap he'd gotten while crewing in the Chicago-Mackinac regatta years ago. Along with the old Aquastar diving watch, it was one of his few prized possessions, and he held on to the brim tightly as Raj gunned the little boat across the water.

"All in a day's work, eh, *machang*?" Upali shouted over

the motor, using the Sinhala term for "mate."

"It never felt this hard when we were doing site surveys up in Lake Superior!" Tusker replied, pausing to smear a forearm across his damp brow.

"But at least there's no risk of frostbite here!" Upali said. They both laughed.

"The legend lives on, from the Chippewa on down, of the big lake they call Gitche Gumee…" Upali broke into song, starting an off-key rendition of "The Wreck of the *Edmund Fitzgerald*." Tusker joined in and they belted out the rest of Gordon Lightfoot's famous song about the sinking of a ship in Lake Superior. Raj watched them with an amused grin.

At the dock, the three of them loaded a rickety cart and pushed it slowly up the dock, its rusty steel wheels protesting under the weight of the scuba tanks, weight belts, and the soaking-wet gear.

It hadn't been an entirely bad day. After lunch, Upali had identified a promising patch of sea bed with his probing. Digging down a couple of feet had turned up some rusty objects of indeterminate age that they had hauled topside and placed in the bottom of a plastic bucket full of sea water. It might just be a jumble of decades-old fishing tackle, but to expose it directly to air would risk rapid oxidation and disintegration, and Upali wanted to get it back to the lab to examine more closely.

Raj had a shed across the busy road from the harbor. It

was five o'clock now, and inside it was dark and smelled of rotten fish. Raj flicked on a naked fluorescent tube light that swayed from the tin ceiling and the sudden light scattered a few large insects. Tusker's skin, despite being bathed in sweat, went instantly cold. He hated the cockroaches, centipedes, and large spiders that lived in the tropics, and even after five months of daily sightings, his phobia hadn't diminished. So much for exposure therapy. Raj grinned, his teeth bright red from the betel nut he constantly chewed. He said something to Upali in Sinhala, who laughed loudly in response.

"Raj wonders how a big guy like you can be so afraid of small critters," Upali said. Tusker gave an exaggerated shiver in Raj's direction. Raj didn't speak much English and Tusker's Sinhala was limited to about ten words. They both laughed.

For the next half hour, the three of them worked to clean and stow gear. Wetsuits were hung to dry, though they never would in the humidity. Tusker turned his neoprene booties inside out and hung them on nails in the wall, away from the scorpions and centipedes that sought their damp crevices at night.

"*Machang*, you should come across to Batti and we'll dive the *Hermes*," Upali finally broke the silence of their chores. "You can't leave Sri Lanka without diving its best wreck. Otherwise you'll think all our diving is like the harbor here!"

"Yeah, I might just take you up on that," Tusker replied. "I'll have to see if my boss will give me a day or two off."

He winked.

"I'll think about it." Upali smiled back. "But only if you haul the tanks."

Raj filled the air compressor with diesel and pulled the starter cord. It roared to life. Tusker fitted the manifold to two of the day's empty air cylinders and made sure the intake hose was rigged up over the top of the shed's swinging door. It had to be far enough away from the compressor's exhaust to not push exhaust fumes and carbon monoxide into the tanks. Not that the air outside the shed was much better, with the passing Leyland buses belching black exhaust that settled in a haze over the road.

Tusker waved to Raj. "Go home! We can finish up here!" Upali nodded and repeated it in Sinhala. Raj looked at both of them, then pressed his palms together, gathered up his sarong, and headed off down the roadside into the gathering dusk. He had three bus connections to make before he'd be home to his wife and two sons, up in the hills behind Galle town, at least an hour's commute.

Tusker switched the compressor manifold to two more tanks and settled onto a flimsy folding chair. He pulled two warm Lion lagers out of the cooler and passed one to Upali. They both sat, not talking over the din of the compressor, and watched the evening traffic pass by.

Tusker thought about the artifacts they'd pulled out of the sea bed and dragged the water-filled bucket close to him. He fumbled for the camping headlamp he kept in his backpack and switched it on. He pulled the

largest object, a curved piece of dark wood that had a
small rusted metal hasp on one end, carefully out of the
saltwater bath. It looked to be a piece of a larger ring and
was quite heavy.

"What do you reckon?" he said to Upali. "Sail hoop?"

The object reminded him of the hoops used to raise
canvas sails on the masts of tall ships. Tusker had seen
plenty of them, still intact, on the schooner wrecks of
Lakes Huron and Michigan. He knew he shouldn't
fiddle too much before sending these to the lab for
proper preservation and analysis, but he couldn't resist
a closer look.

"Don't mess with it too much, *machang*," Upali said,
knowing that Tusker, while a skilled archaeologist, was
also impatient. "We can get it cleaned up in the lab when
I'm back in Colombo."

"A little cleaning won't hurt," Tusker said, grinning. He
examined the hoop more closely in the white light of
his headlamp. He was convinced it was a piece of sail
hoop now, but how old? It was hard to tell. The level of
degradation on this one, even in the salty, polluted harbor,
made it seem much older than that. On the reinforcement
near the hasp he thought he could make out a pattern
beneath the rust.

Tusker pulled a folding knife from his soggy cargo
short pocket and flicked it open. He lightly scraped the
rust away and re-aimed his headlamp's white beam.
Was that…?

"Yup, crow's foot!" Tusker exclaimed. The marking on the metal hasp was a *pheon*, the so-called crow's foot or king's mark, indicating Crown property. The symbol had been engraved or painted on everything from fasteners and cannonballs to rifles and watch dials since the 1300s.

"This is British Royal Navy all right," he said and handed it to Upali, who studied it.

"I think you're right," Upali said, gently setting it back into the bucket of saltwater. "That makes today's efforts worth it for sure. And with any luck, what I find out East next week will be even more exciting."

"Hey man, be careful over there," Tusker's tone turned serious. "Those wrecks are deep."

"Don't worry, *machang*. I'll be back here cracking the whip on you jokers before you know it."

They both laughed, their laughter quickly drowned out by the roar of a passing bus on the dark road outside.

Into the *Vampire*

Bay of Bengal, eight nautical miles east of Batticaloa, Sri Lanka.
Two days later.

Three hundred and thirty-five feet beneath the Indian
Ocean, the blinding arc of a Broco cutting torch lit up
the black water like an exploding star in deep space.
Rory Aitkens squinted behind the dark welding glass
of his dive helmet, intent on his task. He'd been at it for
over two hours, making slow progress. He and McElroy
had spent the first hour of the dive making a survey of
the wreck site, first with a measuring tape, then slowly
swimming along the upturned hull with a Geiger counter.
After they had marked the hull with phosphorescent
chalk, Aitkens took over with the torch.

Aitkens had learned his very specialized skills in the
North Sea. The son of a rig worker, he'd grown up seeing
no other way of life than working the oil fields. By the
age of 19, he was cleaning sewage outlet pipes and
inspecting ships' hulls in Aberdeen. Then, the next 15
years he spent welding pipes and replacing valves at 80
fathoms for £600 a day. When his father died in 2001 in
the *Norskoil Deepstar* platform explosion, Aitkens got a
sizable inheritance from his will. He quit his day job and
spent the next years bleeding away his bank account

on expensive wristwatches and Aberdeen's numerous prostitutes, occasionally taking odd diving gigs that interested him and paid well.

The torch burned at 10,000 degrees Fahrenheit, cutting a white hot line into the three-inch-thick steel plating, which glowed orange and then quickly dulled to a black bruise. Aitkens was making good progress, though a little slower than planned. Turns out, a ship's hull designed to resist torpedoes also does a good job against a cutting torch. He'd have the twelve-by-eight-foot rectangular hole opened up within the hour.

The torch sputtered and died suddenly, and the ocean went immediately black.

"Oh-two's lost pressure!" Aitkens said in an annoyed Scottish brogue that was made even less comprehensible by the effects of the helium gas on his voice. At this depth, divers breathe a blend of 80 percent helium and 20 percent oxygen, known as "heliox." The helium replaces all of the nitrogen in normal air to eliminate its narcotic effects. Heliox provides a clear mind but does have its drawbacks: Helium causes the vocal cords to vibrate faster, raising the voice's pitch to a comical tone. It also carries warmth away from the body faster, hence the hot water that circulated through Aitkens' suit.

"Sorry, pressure regulator glitch," a tinny reply came back down through 100 meters of water. Dive Control onboard DSV *Depth Charge* was monitoring the entire dive via an audio feed of all divers and the cameras inside the bell and on the divers' helmets.

McElroy, waiting on the sea bed nearby, heard the exchange, and chimed in through his own helmet's radio, "Topside, you asleep at the wheel, or what?"

Aitkens chuckled, "We should've gotten paid by the hour!" No reply from above, so Aitkens thought better of continuing.

A few minutes later, the high-pressure oxygen feed from the surface resumed. "Should be good now, Rory," Dive Control squawked. Aitkens squeezed the trigger and sparked the torch back to life.

After another 45 minutes of cutting, the plate, which now resembled a burned outline, hung by a mere few inches of uncut plate on each end. Aitkens had intentionally left these retaining tabs in place so the heavy section of hull wouldn't fall inwards too quickly and crush what lay below it.

"I'm about done," he announced. "Another couple of cuts and she'll collapse in."

"What are you waiting for?" came Rausing's voice over the radio, sounding impatient. Rausing had lured the dive team to Sri Lanka with the promise of an easy job and good money: $25,000 each for this one night's work, plus a bit of decompression time. And for their silence.

Aitkens was about to reply with something snarky but then thought better of it. No point in pissing off the boss. By next Monday he'd be in Bangkok's red light district, where the girls were prettier and they washed your dick when they were done.

Aitkens lit the torch again and slowly sliced through the last small tabs of steel. The 75-year-old metal shrieked in one final protest, then hinged on itself and disappeared down into the black hold of the *Vampire*. A cloud of silt billowed up from inside.

"Still pretty silty," McElroy said a minute later, shining his headlamp into the eerie cloud, "but I'm going in." The view through his helmet faceplate reminded him of driving in a blizzard during a Scottish winter, with visibility barely the length of his outstretched arm.

McElroy tentatively climbed down into the maw. Dive Control could only hear his breathing become rapid as he struggled among the debris. Most of it was unrecognizable as anything from a warship from its seven decades decaying underwater. The bulkhead to his right had partially collapsed in and with it, what appeared to be a shelf unit or rack that had spilled its contents into a jumbled pile that McElroy slipped on as he made his way. Artillery shells? Pipework? Bottles? He tried to discern by the cylindrical shapes he felt with his booted feet. It occurred to him that it might be unexploded ordnance and tried to tread lightly on the debris.

After a half-minute of heavy breathing, McElroy finally spoke. "I don't see the cargo," his Scottish-accented, helium-distorted voice came through. "It's a mess in here, shit everywhere."

"Whatever it takes," came the reply. It was Rausing's

35

voice. McElroy could picture him standing in Dive Control, arms folded. "Given its size, it's most likely fallen to the very bottom of the room."

Easy for you to say. McElroy picked his way down, further into the jagged, twisted obstacle course that conspired to entangle him. He knew what he was looking for. Rausing had prepared them for this, with archival photos, ship's plans, and sketches.

Then he saw it, lying on top of what used to be a stack of wooden crates, now long since disintegrated into rubble that would crumble at the slightest touch. It looked like a cartoon drawing of a bomb, with a bulbous nose and tail fins. It was about the size of his prized 1972 Mini Cooper back home in Dundee, McElroy thought, momentarily amused. *Probably weighs as much too.*

He located two lifting rings on what would have been the top of the bomb, unfurled two large yellow JW Automarine lift bags, and clipped one to each ring. Then he held a pneumatic hose underneath the bags' open ends. He carefully puffed gas into each one until they evenly inflated, lifting the heavy, bulbous cylinder from its resting place. As it rose from the bottom, it dislodged a cloud of silt that rendered McElroy blind. According to plan, Aitkens was waiting outside the wreck, ready to secure the lift cable that snaked down from a powerful hoist onboard the *Depth Charge*.

"Ach, I'm having trouble seeing in here," came McElroy's voice. He sounded rattled.

"Calm yourself, McElroy." Rausing's voice again, with no measure of reassurance, only a command. He abhorred incompetence and fear, especially if either got in the way of his goals. Then, to Aitkens: "Can you reach the cargo yet?"

"Negative," Aitkens replied, "It's still too deep inside."

Before Rausing could reply, there was a muffled cry and McElroy's panicked, helium-inflected voice cut in. "I've slipped down the hold and somehow wedged my foot in something."

The bomb was now above him, slightly buoyant under its lift bags. McElroy looked around through the settling silt, trying to get his bearings. The funhouse effect of the tilted shipwreck played tricks with his perception and he tried to slow his breathing to reorient himself.

He'd lost traction on the loose debris in the steeply pitched bilge and slid 15 feet to what had been the far bulkhead of the bomb room. *How did I fall so far?* He felt his heavily booted foot wedged between a row of pipes that somehow had remained mounted to the bulkhead. His umbilical was stretched taut, fouled on something, making his maneuvering more difficult. He gave his foot a twist, first one way, then the other. The boot didn't budge an inch.

Aitkens peered through the gap in the ship's hull. The interior of the wreck was now zero visibility, the silt McElroy had dislodged billowing out of the hole in the hull in a slow moving cloud.

"I need to go help McElroy," Aitkens said, now also in a mild panic.

"Don't concern yourself with McElroy!" Rausing's voice was pitched now. "Your job is to secure the cargo!"

But by now there was no chance of finding either the bomb or McElroy in the whiteout. Aitkens perched, paralyzed by indecision and growing fear, listening to McElroy's struggling through the radio in his helmet. It sounded as though he was hyperventilating, dangerous at this depth, breathing heliox.

"Get a grip, Mac!" Aitkens shouted to his partner. "You've got plenty of gas, so just calm down and figure it out." No reply, besides more tortured breathing and grunting from McElroy.

At the surface, dawn was showing itself on the horizon. Malcolm Rausing looked out the port side window of the *Depth Charge*'s Dive Control station and frowned. The big Rolex on his wrist read 5:15. The delays at the bottom had pushed them towards daylight. Soon they'd have company. The fishermen returning to Batticaloa would not present a big problem. These were simple men scraping out a living, and the sight of a modern ship offshore wouldn't seem that unusual with the big harbor project going on. The *Depth Charge* wouldn't be new to them either. It had been in the harbor on and off for months, as one of many foreign vessels and companies in the country to take advantage of Sri Lanka's influx of Chinese investments. Still, it only took one fisherman's gossip to raise questions.

How could this go so wrong when I planned so carefully?
wondered Rausing. Three hundred and fifty feet below,
two divers were outside of the bell, panicking, and one
more, Murray, inside. The trip up from the depths would
take time, as would their decompression. If Aitkens
couldn't fetch the bomb, they would have to come out
here a second time to dive the *Vampire*. *It is time we don't
have.* Rausing slammed his fist onto the metal desk in
Dive Control. It was an uncharacteristic loss of control,
and the others in the room looked warily at him.

I knew I should have done the dive myself. But these men had
come on good recommendation—discreet, professional.
Now things were falling apart. Suddenly, above the usual
electronic whines and rumble of the ship came a new
noise: the baritone thrumming of a diesel engine. In a
few steps, Rausing bounded up the metal stairs to the
pilothouse. Captain Kovács lowered his binoculars.

"We've got company."

Rausing grabbed the binoculars, a high-powered Leica
set, and scanned the horizon. In the growing light of the
tropical dawn, Rausing caught sight of a boat moving
slowly up the coastline from the south. It was not one of
the ramshackle fishing boats he'd expected, but a modern
cabin cruiser with a flying bridge and wide, low transom.
There were dive tanks strapped to the railings at the back.
It was still a couple of miles off but would be on them in
ten minutes. Would they pass by? He raised the binoculars
again. This time he made out the Sri Lankan flag painted
on the bow along with the name "R/V *Taprobane*." A
government research vessel. *Damn it.* He had to act, fast.

Rausing picked up the radio to Dive Control. "Raise the bell," he said matter-of-factly. He was met with silence, then it crackled back, "Ah, sir, McElroy and Aitkens…"

"I said, raise the bell. Don't question me again."

"Yes, sir," came a stammered reply.

"Diver 1, get into the bell immediately. Bell diver, switch off Diver 2 and… cut."

Inside the bell, Murray raised his eyebrows and shook his head. *Wow, ruthless*, he thought, then stood up and shimmied around the steel grid platform at the perimeter of the bell to a series of valves marked *Diver 1* and *Diver 2*.

In the depths, Aitkens had heard the exchange and gave one last look in the direction of McElroy, who was invisible now behind the wall of silt. Then he turned and pulled himself hand-over-hand up his umbilical as fast as he could so he'd not be ripped up off the bottom by the ascending bell.

McElroy was in full panic but no one heard him now. Dive Control had shut off his helmet radio. He pleaded and cajoled into the empty microphone as he tugged at his trapped foot.

Inside the bell, Murray reached for the big handle marked *Diver 2* and pulled it perpendicular to the direction of flow. *Off*. Then he grabbed a hacksaw that was hanging on the wall only for the most extreme emergencies. With a few quick strokes the umbilical fell away out of the bell just as a horrified Aitkens pulled himself up the ladder.

In the pilothouse, a voice came over the radio on the public Channel 16. "DSV *Depth Charge*, this is R/V *Taprobane*, do you read?" Captain Kovács reached for the mouthpiece but Rausing grabbed it first.

"This is *Depth Charge*," he said in a mild, almost friendly voice. "Good morning."

"Morning," came the reply. "Looks like you're running without lights over there. A bit dangerous." It was a Sri Lankan's voice, with good English.

"Thanks for letting us know," Rausing replied, while gesturing to Kovács to switch on the running lights. "An oversight on our part, sorry."

The voice came back. "What are you guys doing so far offshore? I thought you were working on the harbor project?"

"We just came out for some fresh air last night," Rausing said, "the air in the harbor is so stuffy, we thought we'd anchor out here for a change."

"OK..." the voice sounded confused. "Well, we're out here for some sonar sweeps and you guys are in our search area. How much longer are you planning to take in the fresh air?"

"We'll be gone in a few minutes," Rausing replied, "just doing some final tweaks to our hoist in open water."

"Got it," came the *Taprobane*, "we'll stay out of your way til you leave. Have a good day."

"And to you, Captain....?"

"Karuna, Upali Karuna. I'm no boat captain. I'm with the Ministry of Culture, History, and Archaeology."

"Looking for anything interesting out here? Some sunken treasure perhaps?" Rausing gave a brittle laugh. "Or I suppose you aren't allowed to say."

"We're trying to locate a World War II ship that went down around here. No treasure, I'm afraid." Karuna chuckled.

"Well, good luck to you and your crew. We'll be out of your way shortly." Rausing clicked off and frowned. *Job incomplete, and now, interference.* He turned to the captain, his eyes noticeably darker with suppressed anger. "As soon as the bell is up, we move," he instructed and walked out of the pilothouse.

Inside the *Vampire*, Gus McElroy suddenly felt his umbilical go slack. His helmet lights died—total darkness. Then he couldn't get a breath. No gas! Had his umbilical fouled when he fell into the hold? He fumbled for his bailout supply valve and twisted it open, feeling a fresh rush of gas into his helmet. But he wouldn't have long. These tanks were only good for about 15 minutes, less with exertion and panic.

He pulled against the pipes that trapped his ankle. It was no use. The boot was stuck fast in the gap. *Stay calm, Gus, stay calm. They'll come to help you soon. A hacksaw to cut the pipes, yes, that's what he needed! Rory wouldn't just leave me.*

Three hundred fifty feet above him, the diving bell surfaced in a great cascade of water, the crane pulling it aboard through the moon pool. The sun had finally poked above the surface of the Indian Ocean to the east, and on the horizon the first fishing boats were motoring in with their night's bounty to sell at the market in Batticaloa.

The bell would be mated to the onboard habitat chamber, where the divers would transfer for their decompression. It would now be even more comfortable with one less diver in the cramped compartment. The big diesels of the *Depth Charge* came to life and the ship swung around to sail west, towards the coast.

Sound carries well underwater, far better than in air. Gus McElroy could hear a distant rumble and wondered for a moment what it was. An engine? *It couldn't be!* He had only a few minutes of gas left in his bailout bottle, maybe less with his fast, panicked breathing. His booted foot remained stuck in the piping. He had a sudden idea. If he could wriggle out of his dive suit, he could pull his foot free and swim out! In the dark, he felt for the latches for his helmet and unsnapped them. The cold ocean flooded in, causing him to gasp, inhaling water. He resisted coughing and held his breath while he unzipped the suit and struggled out of it.

He felt his foot pop out of the suit's integrated boot and the tangled suit fell away. He was free! His lungs were burning now with the buildup of carbon dioxide, and the saltwater burned and blinded his eyes. He smashed into something hard—the bomb—which was knocked off of its neutrally buoyant perch beneath the lift bags and crashed down past him. He paid it no attention. He had to get out of the ship! He hadn't considered how he'd make it to the surface. His fight or flight instinct was in full bloom.

McElroy swam in a wild, flailing butterfly crawl inside the dark tomb. His diaphragm spasmed and he fought against the urge to inhale until, in a final primal human reflex, he opened his mouth and took a deep breath of cold sea water. His body drifted down, settling next to his empty dive suit and helmet. The *Vampire* had claimed its tenth victim.

The *Taprobane*

Bay of Bengal, eight nautical miles east of Batticaloa, Sri Lanka. The same day.

In the morning, before dawn, Upali Karuna and his small team—a boat captain, a sonar expert, and a young intern—loaded up a small dive skiff from Sebastian de Silva's Deep Blue Resort and motored out to the R/V *Taprobane* where she was anchored offshore, beyond Batticaloa's shallow lagoon. There they hefted a sonar device, hundreds of feet of coaxial cable, and a rather expensive remotely operated vehicle aboard and set off to search for a shipwreck.

The research vessel *Taprobane* was a 46-foot former navy patrol boat, with a wide aft deck, a broad forward cabin, and plenty of storage below deck. When the Ministry of Culture, History and Archaeology had acquired it from the Sri Lankan Navy after the end of the civil war, they'd refitted it for use as a sonar boat that could serve as a platform for divers. Its camouflaged hull had been painted white and adorned with MOCHA's official seal, the Sri Lankan flag on both sides of the bow, and her name emblazoned across the low stern.

Upali stood on the forward deck of the boat, enjoying the

predawn breeze and a flask of hot milk tea he'd brought from the Deep Blue. The sky was just starting to turn orange on the horizon. Upali wanted to get an early start, since launching the ROV off of the transom was heavy work that would only be made worse in a blazing midday sun. They'd reach the search coordinates by about 6:00.

"Hold up, Ranjith!" Upali called over his shoulder to the captain. "We've got a vessel in our grid area. Toss me those binocs." The *Taprobane* slowed to a crawl, its twin Mercury Marine diesels reduced to a loping rumble. Looking through the binoculars in the dim light, Upali made out a massive ship with no running lights. It looked out of place there, a huge slab of steel where, at most, he might have expected to spot a wooden fishing trawler. Upali squinted. He could just make out two figures in the pilothouse, silhouetted against the eerie green light of navigation instruments. From their stance, they were clearly looking back at the *Taprobane*.

As he scanned the ship from bow to stern, Upali recognized the distinctive high superstructure at the front and the low-slung rear deck pierced by the tall skeleton of a powerful crane. It was the dive support vessel he'd seen in Batticaloa harbor, the *Depth Charge*. But what were they doing out this far? He'd only seen the ship in the gouged-out basin of the forthcoming deep water port, where its divers were presumably at work fitting pipe or electrical cabling. Otherwise it had always been tied up along the makeshift pier overnight, its crew staying aboard. Were they in trouble? Some sort of power outage causing them to drift and lose their lights? He'd better raise them on the radio.

"DSV *Depth Charge*, this is R / V *Taprobane*, do you read?"

By 6:00, the *Depth Charge* had moved off. Upali watched it aim for Batticaloa harbor, exhaust trailing behind. "Fresh air..." he murmured, shaking his head. Ranjith guided the *Taprobane* into position for their search, his eyes on the GPS screen, hands on the wheel and throttle.

Shipwreck hunting has a romantic sound to it, largely thanks to tales of Caribbean treasure hunts and Clive Cussler novels, but in reality, it is stupefyingly boring. The first step is to identify anomalies on the ocean floor, those features that don't appear to be naturally occurring objects such as rocks, coral heads, or schools of fish. This is done by dragging a side-scan sonar device behind the boat in a systematic pattern, a process known as "mowing the lawn," and is just about as exciting as walking up and down a suburban backyard. The sonar device, known as a tow fish, is shaped like a torpedo, with a cylindrical body and stabilizing fins at its back end. As it moves through the water, the tow fish sends audio pulses into the depths, which bounce back off the sea bed. This paints a sort of electronic picture of the terrain on a laptop screen on the boat. Man-made objects, usually shipwrecks or pieces of debris, are recognizable by their more geometric shapes on the screen. Right angles and straight lines rarely occur in nature. These anomalies are marked with GPS coordinates, to be investigated more thoroughly later with the ROV. A day spent mowing the lawn under the tropical sun, watching a computer monitor for anomalies, is only tolerable with the promise of actually finding something, which rarely happens.

A few weeks earlier, a fisherman had snagged his line on what he assumed was a rock ledge and pulled up a faded orange life ring with some indistinguishable writing on it. A shipwreck? That would explain the good fishing. Fish tend to congregate around wrecks for their relative shelter on barren sea floors, but there were no known wrecks in this area. Word got back through the fish market gossip, on up to a local politician, who alerted the naval base in Trincomalee. The navy didn't have the time to go on wreck hunts, so it passed the message on to MOCHA's offices in Colombo, and that's how Upali Karuna found himself slowly motoring up the coast on the *Taprobane* on this cool morning.

After an hour and a half of mowing the lawn, the MOCHA team decided to investigate a promising anomaly from the sonar scans, a long shadow on the slope of a deep ocean trench that slashes in from the continental shelf towards Batticaloa. Here the sea deepens from 150 feet to over 300 quickly, and then drops over a precipice into 2,000 feet of dark water.

"We're here," Ranjith said, cutting the engine. "Drop anchor now!" Deepa, the intern, threw the anchor off the bow and stepped aside as the chain and heavy rope unspooled into the water.

On the transom, the sonar man, Suresh, squatted over the ROV, a small robot about the size of an office copy machine. Tethered to the boat by a long, thick umbilical for power and controls, it could drop into the depths, illuminate the darkness with a quiver of powerful lights, and capture what it saw with a high-definition camera. Despite his rather nautical job at MOCHA, Suresh was not much for boats and had never learned to swim. But he was an expert in underwater electronics like the ROV, having interned at Woods Hole in America and worked on the R/V *Petrel* when it had discovered several important World War II wrecks in the Pacific a few years earlier.

"She's ready to splash," Suresh said, giving one last tug on the cable connection as if to prove his point. He and Upali lifted the robot by its bottom skids and shuffled to the edge of the transom. "Bon voyage, little friend," Suresh said as it splashed into the water and disappeared below the surface.

Upali and Suresh settled in at the computer monitor inside the forward cabin. The screen showed a direct feed from the camera on the front of the ROV as it descended through 300 feet of ocean: darkness, with the occasional cloud of drifting particulate reflected in the craft's 10,000-lumen floodlights. Deepa hovered over their shoulders. This was her first fieldwork as a MOCHA intern, and she was excited at the prospect of actually finding something. Ranjith sat on the transom, smoking.

"We should have hit bottom by now, eh?" Upali said. The ROV's depth gauge showed 357 feet.

"Well, according to the charts, we're literally on the edge of the dropoff, so if we overshot by even a few feet, we'd be over the side in very deep water," Suresh said. "Let me alter the heading a bit and bring her back up a ways." He pulled on the joystick delicately with his fingertips. The depth reading changed, despite the continuous blackness on screen. *342, 337…*

"Whoa, what's that?" Deepa's finger darted out, poking the monitor. They all leaned in. The video feed clearly showed a twisted procession of railing stanchions atop a coral-encrusted slab of steel. The ROV had come up almost beneath it. Suresh cursed and quickly maneuvered to avoid entangling the umbilical cable. *Must be the bow,* Upali thought.

"Follow that railing," Upali said. "To the right must be aft." Suresh didn't answer, but the view on the monitor, with its wide-angle lens, zoomed along the upper hull of the ship, encrusted with hard and soft corals and the occasional waving sea fan. Then, something unmistakable. A cannon. "We've got ourselves a warship." Upali leaned back and smiled. "I'd bet a round of beers that this is the *Vampire.*"

"We got very lucky," said Suresh, not taking his eyes from the screen. "She's literally hanging over a cliff. A few more feet to the north and this wreck would be in 2,000 feet of water."

"A little beyond your diving depth, eh, *machang*?" Upali elbowed him in the ribs and laughed.

For the next several hours, they scoured the wreck with the ROV, methodically working from forward to aft, breaking for lunch and, later, some tea. By late afternoon, they still hadn't found any evidence that positively identified this ship as the *Vampire*, but Upali was sure that it was. The old war records and British Admiralty charts showed no other shipwrecks in this area, and judging from its size and armaments, it was clearly a destroyer. To know for sure, Upali would compare the footage from the ROV to the photos and engineering drawings he had of the *Vampire* back at the Deep Blue. He was ready to call it a day. They'd be back out tomorrow with more definite surveying goals. Upali pulled out his phone and dashed off a cryptic message: "Think we've found Dracula." He smiled. Tusker would be so jealous.

"Hey, come look at this," Suresh called from the monitor. Upali yawned and came back inside. "There's a perfectly rectangular hole in the hull here. There's no sea life growing around it either. Almost looks… fresh."

There, on the monitor, was a wide maw into the ship's hold, outlined in a black jagged rectangle. It couldn't be from a torpedo or explosion of any kind. "Maybe a hatch that came free when she sank?" Suresh mused.

"No, not there. That's below the water line. I've never seen anything like that," Upali replied. "Can you get inside there safely?"

"Shouldn't be too hard," Suresh said, tweaking the joystick. The ROV responded. "That hole is big enough for a car to drive through."

Inside was a jumble of debris, covered in seven decades of silt, unrecognizable. Upali gasped aloud. What a treasure trove for an archaeologist—a time capsule unseen since World War II. Suddenly, a bright object appeared on the monitor, so out of place it caused the two men to jump. It was yellow, spherical, and reflected back the white light of the ROV lamps. As Suresh moved the craft in closer, Upali leaned in and squinted. He could make out writing. He mouthed the words, "Kirby Morgan..."

"It's a dive helmet!" he shouted, recognizing the famous maker of commercial diving gear. This was a saturation diver's helmet, no question, and not the kind used for salvaging wrecks long ago. No, this was the kind of helmet seen on modern commercial divers welding oil pipeline and laying cable in the North Sea, the Gulf of Mexico... or Batticaloa harbor.

Upali's skin went cold. The *Depth Charge*. That explained the fresh hole in the hull, the doused running lights, the nighttime anchorage. Were they cutting up the *Vampire* for her higher-carbon steel, which would fetch millions on the market? But that sort of clandestine poaching was typically done by ill-outfitted amateurs in shallower waters, not a commercial diving company in over 300 feet of water. He'd have to report this to the police. No—the Sri Lankan Navy.

"All right, shut her down," he said. "Let's get back. We may have gotten into something a little deeper than our old shipwreck."

Night Moves

Bay of Bengal, one mile offshore of Batticaloa.
2:48am the next morning.

The Zodiac bounced across the light swells, following the coastline. The two men in the *Depth Charge*'s rigid inflatable said nothing to each other, even as the sound of the motor raised a nearby school of dolphins, which arced out of the water as if to play. Scholz glanced at their silvery backs and then turned away again, training his eyes forward. To the west, the Batticaloa lighthouse stood impotent in the dark, its light long since extinguished.

The man at the back cut the outboard motor and the boat coasted to a sloshing stop. The only sound now was the distant roar of the surf breaking over the sandbar at the entrance of the lagoon. The handsome white cruiser lay at anchor ahead of them, about 200 yards away, a single white light atop its cabin illuminated for safety.

Scholz, perched at the bow of the Zodiac, was almost sure no one would be aboard at this hour, but he pulled a night vision scope out of a black duffel and scanned just to be certain. He tossed it back in the bag and nodded to the man at the motor, who wore a thin black rash guard of the type tropical surfers wore for sun protection.

But here, in the wee hours of a Sri Lankan morning, he wore it for a different reason. In the humid air, his face glistened with sweat.

Scholz, who was wearing a black, two-millimeter hooded wetsuit, pulled on a pair of Scubapro Jet Fins and spat into a diving mask. He rubbed the glass with two fingers to keep it from fogging, rinsed it in the sea, hoisted an aluminum scuba cylinder and harness onto the Zodiac's gunwale, secured his mask, bit down on his regulator's mouthpiece, and backrolled into the water with only a small splash. He'd done this sort of thing before.

Bobbing to the surface, he held up the large bubble compass strapped to his wrist. He aligned the lubber line with the white boat in the distance, then signaled to the other man, who lifted a large rolltop drybag from the bottom of the Zodiac and handed it over the side. Scholz sank out of sight. After a few seconds, a trail of bubbles on the surface marked his progress straight towards his target.

At around 3:00 in the morning, Upali Karuna awoke with a start. He lay on the hard mattress in his room at the Deep Blue Resort, his senses alert. Had Suresh said something? He listened. All he heard was the rhythmic breathing of his roommate in the next bed over and the ticking of the ceiling fan above him in the dark. Must have been a car backfiring, or maybe a mosquito in his ear. Might as well have a piss. He quietly got up and padded across the concrete floor to the bathroom.

Without turning on the light, he found his way over to the toilet, raised the seat and let go, enjoying the sweet relief. They'd celebrated their finding with a little too much beer in the Deep Blue's dining area.

Through the open window of the bathroom he heard a motor in the distance, as if carrying across water. An outboard? The *Taprobane* was anchored offshore and though theft from boats wasn't common here, he was glad they brought the ROV and sonar equipment ashore every night.

His mind turned to the *Depth Charge* and the meeting he'd be having in a few hours up in Trincomalee with the navy lieutenant. He'd been vague on the phone when he scheduled the meeting. He wanted to make one more visit to the *Vampire* with the ROV before he presented his evidence, just to be certain.

The sound of the motor stopped, replaced by the buzzing and clicking of a million nocturnal insects outside. He flushed the toilet and crept back to his bed. He was asleep within two minutes.

By watching the luminous minute hand of his diving watch, Scholz knew how far he'd swum. He slowed and looked up, 15 feet to the surface. Despite the lack of moonlight, he could see the waves and the large silhouette of a boat. Slowly rising, he broke the surface near the stern. The waves slapped lazily against the hull and the automatic bilge pump piddled out a stream of water and then shut off.

He slipped off his black fins and set them on the boat's transom, then silently climbed out of the water, setting his tank and harness down in one motion. He paused to assess the open rear deck of the boat: no one aboard and the engine hatch right where he had been told it would be. He knelt and opened it, then unsealed the drybag he'd brought, pulling out what looked like a small, badly wrapped birthday gift. Except there was a tangle of wires protruding from one end, plugged into a cheap Casio digital watch.

Scholz unclipped a small torch from his harness and aimed its beam at the watch's dial. He glanced at his own wristwatch and then fiddled with the Casio's buttons. Rausing had told him to set the alarm for 7:00. *They'd be on board by then.* He reached down below the Mercury Marine engine and carefully wedged the package under its sump, then closed the hatch with a silent click.

Scholz gave one last look around, rolled up the empty drybag, shouldered his tank, and slipped into the black water at the back of the boat. Then he rotated the bezel of his compass 180 degrees, descended, and swam back the way he came.

Circle of Life

Rampart Inn, Galle Fort, Sri Lanka.
The next day.

Tusker was underwater with Upali, working a dig site. He reached down to probe the sea bed, then saw his arm was bare. No wetsuit. No scuba gear at all. He was holding his breath. He waved his arms to get Upali's attention—*I need your regulator!*—but Upali didn't seem to notice. His friend swam just out of reach. Tusker kicked up, up, up toward the surface, felt his lungs about to burst.

He awoke, gasping, bathed in sweat.

Tusker rubbed his eyes. He'd had the dream before. What did it mean? He was never much for psychoanalysis or dream interpretation, but maybe the universe was trying to tell him something. The fan was buzzing on its stand in the corner. What had woken him?

There was a loud knock on his door. It was Sidath, the guesthouse owner, holding a tray with tea. Back home, Tusker was a coffee drinker, but since coming to Sri Lanka, he preferred what they did best here.

"Your friend, Mr. Walsh, is waiting for you downstairs, sir," Sidath said quietly.

"Thanks, Sidath," he said blearily, clutching his poorly tied sarong in one hand and reaching for the mug with the other. Sidath tipped his head side to side, in the typical South Asian expression that could mean a dozen things, this time, "You're welcome," then turned and padded quietly down the hallway.

Tusker shut the door and took a long draw on the tea. It was strong and sweet with milk, the color of wet clay and utterly delicious. *Odd for Ian to come so early*, thought Tusker, glancing at his watch. With Upali gone for the week, they'd agreed on a later start today. Maybe Ian forgot. *In any case*, Tusker thought, *I've still got time for a shower and my tea. Ian can wait a bit.*

He set the mug down on the small desk, dropped to the floor and hammered out five quick sets of 20 pushups. Though slinging diving gear all day was a workout by itself, Tusker had kept up this routine since college. He hated the gym, and his only steady exercise was pushups and the occasional open-water swim when he had the chance. By the time he was done with the fifth set, his lean, muscled torso glistened with sweat.

He walked over to the window and finished the tea in a few gulps. The fort was waking up. A man pedaled by on a heavy bicycle with an impossibly large load of fish on the back, no doubt the previous night's catch. Tusker's eyes caught those of an older woman in the upstairs apartment across the road, who was hanging wet towels

58

to dry. He smiled at her but she averted her gaze and went back inside. Tusker was still shirtless, and suddenly felt very white and exposed.

When Tusker arrived in Sri Lanka six months ago, Upali had arranged lodging for him in a small guesthouse, the Rampart Inn, on Pedlar Street inside the Galle Fort. The inn was a small two-story building wedged between a trendy cafe and a Buddhist monastery. Just across the road were the sloping grassy ramparts, topped with stone battlements that dropped off to the sea 50 feet below. These ancient fort walls were what saved the residents of the fort from the wall of water that rolled in on Boxing Day, 2004, while most of the rest of Galle town was obliterated. Sidath had owned the Rampart Inn since the 1980s, and it had become a favorite of aid workers and NGOs during the aftermath of the tsunami.

Tusker knew Ian was waiting, but he badly needed a shower, having skipped one last night. The previous day, he'd borrowed a bicycle and ridden down to the resort town of Unawatuna. There he spent the day playing cricket with the local kids, and pounding back Lion lagers at a beach bar until midnight. As he flicked on the anemic fluorescent bulb in the bathroom, he caught movement up near the ceiling. A gecko clung to the wall, its tail flicking. In its mouth was a half-consumed black cockroach, rear legs still twitching. "Circle of life," Tusker said aloud.

He dropped his sarong to the floor and turned on the bathtub's tap. There was no shower curtain and the leaky plastic spray wand was on a hose connected to the spigot.

There was only one handle: cold. Rust-colored water gushed out. When it cleared, Tusker braced himself and stepped into the tub. Now he was awake.

He brushed his teeth and finger-combed an unruly mop of blonde hair away from his forehead. In the mirror, under the fluorescent light and against his deeply tanned face, his eyes looked even more blue. He noticed the creases seemed to be getting more pronounced, and remembered his ex-wife always telling him to wear sunscreen to stay looking young. Can't help things now, he thought, and switched off the bathroom light.

The relative cool of dawn had quickly evaporated, replaced by the sultry heat that would build all day. Tusker hoped they could finish surveying the promising site they'd found last week. It'd be great to finish out his stay in Sri Lanka with a big discovery.

He dressed in a pair of rumpled cotton cargo shorts and one of those supposedly "insect proof" shirts he'd stocked up on before coming to Sri Lanka. He filled his water bottle from a jug in the corner of his room, tucked it in his backpack and headed downstairs. He'd grab a couple of egg hoppers, those delicious thin coconut pancakes unique to Sri Lanka, from the stall next door to take along for breakfast.

Ian was waiting for him in the lobby with a grave face.

"Bad weekend?" Tusker asked. "Did that girl at The Lighthouse shoot you down again?"

Ian ignored his joke. "Took your sweet time getting down here," he said."Upali's dead."

"Well, that's a pretty extreme way to get out of digging in the mud here," Tusker said, smiling. "Come on, let's grab some hoppers and get down to the shed. We found something promising on Friday that I want to show you."

"No, mate, I'm serious. The research boat caught on fire and they're saying no survivors." Ian's eyes were dark and earnest. He held up his iPhone to show a news site's homepage. There was an old file photo of the R/V *Taprobane*, MOCHA's sonar and dive boat. Headline: "Ministry Boat Sunk, No Survivors."

"When did this happen? It has to be a mistake. I got a text yesterday from Upali saying they'd found something." Tusker snatched the phone from Ian's hands and pulled it close to his face, as if looking for some clue that this was a hoax.

"It was early this morning, apparently. I got a call from Dinesh at MOCHA in Colombo an hour ago and came here straightaway," Ian said. "I couldn't quite gather what had happened. He said the boat just suddenly exploded or something. There was a search, fishermen helped and all, but they've found no survivors. Dinesh is driving over to Batti this morning to meet with the police."

Tusker handed the phone back and stared at Ian. "What the hell? That was a pretty new boat. Upali's always safe. I'm going to go over there. You got the van here?"

Ian nodded. "Yeah, outside. I already packed some things. I assumed you'd want to head over there."

Tusker wasn't listening anymore. It was only a few days earlier when he and Upali were diving in Galle harbor and clinking lagers in the shed. Now, gone. It hit him viscerally, like a blow to the back of the head.

The winter when Tusker met Upali was one of the coldest Michigan's Upper Peninsula had faced, the kind where you leave your car running all night so it starts the next morning. Tusker remembered sitting in the archaeology department's lab, looking out the window and seeing this Indian-looking guy repeatedly slipping and falling on the icy sidewalk. He was wearing a cheap parka that was woefully inadequate in the face of the minus-30 windchills.

Tusker loved the winter, relishing the challenge of not only surviving it, but getting out and enjoying its frigid beauty. He and Upali couldn't have been more opposite, but ended up sharing an apartment on campus and became best friends. Upali would always crank up the thermostat when Tusker was away so that when Tusker would return, he'd find Upali studying at the dining table in shorts and a T-shirt. Tusker would turn down the heat and fling open the windows, Upali laughing gleefully. Then he'd do it again the next day.

During the next four years at school, Tusker learned to cook curry and eat spicy foods. Upali learned to ski. Tusker grew to respect Upali for tolerating not only the cold and the chilly drysuit dives in Lake Superior, but also the homogeneous culture of the upper Midwest. By the end of their third year, they were selling curry packets out of the back of Tusker's pickup truck at the farmer's market, a little slice of Sri Lanka in Michigan.

"We can collect our dive gear at the shed and then head out." Ian broke into Tusker's thoughts. "I've phoned ahead to this guy, Sebastian, who runs the Deep Blue, where the MOCHA team was staying. He said we can stay there."

Newly vacant rooms, Tusker thought and grimaced. He was already turning to head back upstairs. "Give me a couple of minutes. I'm going to grab a few things in my room."

The MOCHA van was one of those small Toyota models you see all over the developing world: short wheelbase, a sliding door, the engine under a hump mounted under the middle of the vehicle, not the most pleasant place for a six-hour drive across Sri Lanka. The van was crammed with gear, a cooler, a single dive fin, quart oil bottles, and the repaired dredge pump in the back.

The driver, Srivathnan, was a dark-skinned Tamil man with a big smile. Tusker never could pronounce his name right and called him Nathan. When Tusker came out of the Rampart Inn with his duffel bag, Srivathnan started the engine. Tusker nodded to him and piled in the back.

At the shed, Ian, Tusker, and Raj heaved the pump out of the back of the van, sliding it in next to the bucket of seawater. Tusker saw Ian's quizzical look.

"Friday's findings," he said in reply, "British Navy, I think." Last week's excitement faded, and Tusker had an urge to just dump out the bucket and toss the artifacts back in the harbor. They grabbed damp wetsuits, fins, and buoyancy wings and heaped them in the back of the van. "That's gonna make for a smelly ride," Ian tried to joke. Tusker didn't react.

Srivathnan smoked a cigarette in the shade, talking quietly to Raj. Tusker and Ian finished loading the van and slammed shut the heavy rear door. "Well, Raj, you've got a couple days off til we get back," Tusker said. He could see that Srivathnan had told him the news. Raj's eyes looked watery. He didn't say anything, but touched Tusker's arm and shook his head side to side. Tusker clasped his hand and quickly turned to go. "Come on, Nathan. Long drive ahead."

Deep Salvage

Bay of Bengal, eight nautical miles east of Batticaloa.
15 April, 1942

The Royal Navy dive tender HMS *Drake* arrived in
Trincomalee a week after the *Vampire* sank to the bottom
of the Bay of Bengal. She didn't have far to come. The
Easter raid on Colombo by the Japanese had left that
city's harbor littered with downed planes, sunken
ships and unexploded ordnance. The difficult work of
removing all this debris kept the *Drake's* small team of
clearance divers busy. The shallow water there meant
little risk of the bends, so the divers rotated into the water
in shifts around the clock, only pausing to eat and sleep.
They would have remained there for another month if
the urgent order to move around to the east coast for an
undisclosed mission had not been received from London.

Bodies were still washing up down the coast near the
small fishing village of Pasikudah when the *Drake*
steamed into position offshore. The southeast monsoon
season hadn't yet blown itself out and the surface was
choppy, with uneven swells and whitecaps. The *Drake*
idled over what was thought to be *Vampire's* final resting
place, extrapolated from survivors' dead reckoning and
the heaviest concentration of debris and leaking fuel oil.

The *Drake's* captain, a Welshman named Llewellyn, came out of the pilothouse and surveyed the frothy seas. Among the whitecaps was a calmer radius of water, flattened out by the leaking oil from the wreck below. He turned to the dark-haired man standing in the shade of the ship's foc'sle.

"This is your operation, Lieutenant," he said, studying the impassive eyes. "But 60 fathoms is awfully deep."

The other man, dressed in a navy blue Mackintosh coat against the spray, didn't make eye contact with Llewellyn. "Yes it is, Captain. But needs must." Then he turned and spoke directly. "Your crew has all signed the Official Secrets Act, I trust?"

"Yes, they have, including the divers," the captain replied. "I've put the signed copies in your stateroom." The intelligence officer nodded, turned, and walked aft along the railing with the steadiness of a man who had been to sea many times.

On the broad deck amidships, two men in red watch caps sat in heavy canvas suits while tenders fitted their heavy breastplates, cinched rope to their harnesses and fastened their lead boots. It could have been an ancient scene, squires readying armored knights for battle. Then the copper helmets were ceremonially fitted over their heads. It was difficult work in the uneven seas but the two divers joked with each other right up until their helmets were clicked into place. One tender checked the air hose connections while another confirmed that the wired telephone connection worked, with a tinny "Testing,

1,2,3..." echoing inside the helmets.

The two divers chosen for the job were the most experienced in the Royal Navy, with hundreds of hours of diving between them. One was Lionel Stanwick, a good-humored shipbuilder's son from Newcastle. Growing up around the Swan Hunter shipyard, "Wick," as everyone called him, was well suited for salvage work on sunken ships similar to many built just down the road from his childhood home.

The second diver was a young, sandy-haired man named Angus Rausing. Rausing cut an imposing figure with his broad shoulders, piercing pale eyes, and serious demeanor. He'd learned his craft the hard way, in the cold, dark waters of Scapa Flow in the Orkney Islands. The unpopular son of Swedish immigrant parents, Angus built his own diving helmet out of an old boiler tank and some garden hose and recruited a school mate to crank the pump while he explored the German wrecks that littered the waters around the islands. When the war started, he signed up to be a clearance diver at the age of 17.

The divers and crew knew better than to ask why the *Vampire* took such priority over the larger British ship, *Hermes*. It was an unusual mission to begin with for divers used to clearing munitions and debris from shallow harbors. They were told only to try to gain entry into the bomb room near the stern of the ship and inventory its contents. Then, possibly, a retrieval.

The two men awkwardly climbed down ladders on

the side of the pitching *Drake*. Their lead boots made descending the wet rungs treacherous in the morning swell. A gas compressor on deck was already running, sending air through the hose to the gooseneck fittings at the back of the helmets. With two thumbs down reciprocated from the tenders on deck, the divers stepped backwards into the sea and sank like stones. The tenders watched them descend in a torrent of bubbles, and then returned their eyes to the horizon, scouting for Japanese planes or ships.

The pneumofathometer on the compressor's panel showing the divers' depth went past 300 feet, the accepted limit of what could be safely dived while breathing air, and kept dropping. It stopped at 348 feet. The tenders held tight to the divers' safety ropes and ensured that the air and communication lines didn't get fouled on the *Drake*'s stanchions.

"I've lost communications, sir!" shouted the young seaman manning the two-way telephone. "I'm only getting static. Should we bring them up?" It had been only six minutes since the divers went into the water.

"Leave them another few minutes," the Naval Intelligence officer replied calmly. "If they get into trouble, they know the rope signals." The tenders manning the safety lines looked at each other but stayed quiet. Unbeknownst to them, 350 feet below, one of the divers was in trouble.

Stanwick had landed directly on the upturned hull of the sunken *Vampire*. His lead boots were better suited for walking on the sea floor than on the rounded, smooth hull of a sunken ship and he scrabbled for footing. With a gloved hand, he gripped a railing on the edge of the hull and tugged on it to steady himself. This forced him off balance and he fell to his knees, straining to stay upright.

It was vital when wearing these positive pressure helmets to remain vertical or else they would fill with water. Stanwick was panting with exertion, and with each breath, he was pulling in lungfuls of toxic, compressed oxygen. *Where was Rausing?* Through the tiny porthole, his eyes searched the gloomy darkness for his partner. But he was nowhere in sight.

Angus Rausing had landed forward of the ship's superstructure, touching down almost directly on a searchlight near the starboard railing. The ship was in eerily good condition. The grey paint reflected back his torchlight, and he could see that most of the windows on the pilothouse remained intact. Bubbles emanated from the wreck's bowels, even one week after her sinking. But there was no time to take in the scenery. Rausing knew from the engineering sketches he'd been shown that their target was aft of his current position by at least 20 yards. He had to make his way back along the wreck, no easy feat in his lead boots and heavy suit. He took pains to control his pace and breathing so as not to become hypoxic. The cold of the deep ocean penetrated his suit and woolen undergarments and the sweat on his back from his time at the surface began to chill him.

When Rausing got to Stanwick, the Newcastle man had already blacked out and was lying on his side, his helmet full of water. Rausing called into his helmet's telephone transceiver, but got back only static. He then tried to right Stanwick and purge the helmet, but he was aware of his own exertion and knew there was little he could do to revive Stanwick. He thought about giving the "four tugs" signal on Wick's rope so the tenders could start to pull him up, but then decided not to. They might also pull him up, and he still had a chance to find his target, and that was his strict instruction. Official secrets and all. *No hope for Wick anyway*, he coldly thought. *Might as well get on with the job.*

In the dim yellow cone of his dive torch, he left Wick behind and made his way across the now vertical rear deck of the stricken destroyer to the bulkhead door leading into the bomb room. Everything not attached to the deck now lay below him on the sea floor. Rausing wondered if he would see any dead bodies. Probably not, he guessed. With only nine lost in the sinking, he doubted any would be this far back, in the bomb room, during an aerial attack.

Visualizing the ship's layout, he easily found the bomb room. Entering meant shimmying in sideways, but once inside, he easily walked on what used to be the wall until it opened up into the large space. The sinking had sent the contents of the room down against the upturned inner wall at the far end of the room. In the dim light of his torch, he saw spilled racks of depth charges, crates of 105-millimeter shells and an arsenal of rifles scattered among other debris. He made mental notes of what he saw to report back to the Naval Intelligence man on the *Drake*. There must be something more important in here, he thought. Then he saw it. In the corner was the largest bomb he'd ever seen. It was at least 10 feet long, with a bulbous nose and telltale fins at the back. This was no torpedo. This was meant to be dropped from a plane. *This is what I've been sent for.* No doubt there would be a second dive to retrieve the bomb, but without Wick and no other divers on board the *Drake*, could he do it alone?

Just then, his torch flickered and died. *Flooded, no doubt,* he calmly thought. Rausing found himself in complete blackness. He slowly backpedaled, retracing his steps up the corridor to the outside hatch. The dimmest of ambient light guided him. He didn't panic. He'd been here before, inside a wreck, in the dark. But unlike the old wrecks he dived in Scotland, this one was newly sunk and there was no silt to kick up and obscure his vision, and by pulling on his own air hose he was able to climb back out on to the tilted deck of the *Vampire.*

Somewhere in the dark in front of him was Wick's body. Rausing paused for a moment and then tugged on his safety rope three times to be brought slowly back to the surface. No doubt they would wonder why Wick didn't tug on his rope, but by the time Rausing's decompression was done, they'd have figured it out. *Nothing to be done about it. Wick wasn't that good a diver anyway.*

Rausing's decompression stops would be controlled by the tenders, who watched the pneumofathometer for his depth. He'd be back on the surface in about two hours, which gave him plenty of time to think about what he'd seen inside the *Vampire.* Then, a second dive, possibly even today, to fetch the bomb. *Maybe I'll even be rewarded a medal for valor.* He smiled inside his helmet at the thought as he was slowly reeled upwards.

But there would be no second dive.

Bastard Son

Though he scarcely knew the man, Malcolm Rausing assumed he'd acquired both his affinity for the sea and his taste for violence from his father. Angus Rausing had been discharged from the Royal Navy in 1942 after a diving accident nearly paralyzed him. He was awarded a hardship pension and sent back to Scotland where, after lying low for a few years, he founded a salvage and diving operation, eventually acquiring a fleet of ships that he based in Aberdeen.

Angus was an unforgiving, brutal man, who rewarded loyalty, but punished incompetence, often by medieval means. Once, a long-time employee of Rausing Oceanic, who was suspected of floating a paycheck to pay gambling debts, was found naked in Aberdeen harbor, hypothermic and missing his right hand. Nothing was ever proven about the circumstances of his situation, and the man never spoke of it. He even continued to work for Rausing, rising to the rank of financial controller. But everyone noticed he never looked Angus Rausing in the eye again.

Malcolm was born to a Portuguese mother, Andréa, with whom Angus had spent a month while overseeing a dredging project in the harbor at Cascais. Andréa was an

Iberian beauty, with parchment-colored skin and short black hair that framed high cheekbones and dark brown eyes. Malcolm remembered numerous men passing through the house with regularity, their hands probing and faces hungry, leaving a crumpled wad of cash on his mother's nightstand. He assumed his father had been one of these men, but Andréa told him he was not. "Your father is a very important and powerful man," she would say, which made Malcolm grow to hate him even more.

Though he had no soft spot for children, Angus did possess a sense of responsibility and sent Malcolm's mother a healthy stipend every month until Malcolm turned 18. About once a year he would return, ostensibly on business, and visit the tidy apartment he rented for mother and bastard son. To Malcolm, the man's face was ugly and broad, his eyes piercing, his limp a gruesome remnant of a final dive years before.

On one of these visits, when Malcolm was 12, Angus pulled him down onto a chair and told him he had a secret, one that had almost cost him his life but also could make him rich. His father's breath was laced with whisky, his grip strong. When Malcolm asked him what it was, his father angrily pushed him away. "Why would I tell a bastard like you?" he said, and laughed.

Angus insisted that his son be educated in England, and, when Malcolm turned 14, he was sent to boarding school at Ipswich. By this time, his inherited cruel streak had surfaced, and he was disciplined for fighting four times until the school threw him out after his second year for the particularly vicious beating of a younger boy who

74

simply looked at Malcolm a bit too long.

From there, Malcolm drifted around Europe, selling heroin in France, stealing cars in Belgium, and selling stolen watches in Holland for money. He would occasionally appear at his mother's door, always leaving her a little bit of cash before he would disappear a week later. She never asked him what he did.

On one of Malcolm's visits to Cascais, he came home from a night of drinking to find a man shouting at his mother. He was an old john, a fat, rich Spaniard who'd occasionally employed Andréa's services. His belt was undone, a bottle in his hand. Malcolm could see that his mother had been crying. He snatched the bottle from the man, smashed it across his head and used the jagged butt of it to castrate him. If his mother hadn't intervened, Malcolm would have killed the man.

Malcolm served four years in a Lisbon prison. His sentence would have been longer if the man he'd beaten had not been a Spanish diplomat who wanted to keep the whole episode quiet.

Prison taught Malcolm about power dynamics, and how to clamp down his fighting fury into a more controlled seething. He emerged stoic and brooding. The violence was still there, but harnessed, exercised only when necessary and useful. The day he was discharged, he found out that his father had died, leaving Rausing Oceanic entirely to his bastard son.

The company was nearly bankrupt when Malcolm

arrived at its offices in Aberdeen, fresh out of prison. His father had over-leveraged on new ships in the expectation of an oil boom that never materialized. Bestowing the failing firm to Malcolm seemed like a cruel, final joke.

The knowledge gained from a lifetime living by his wits, his ruthless efficiency, and an almost psychopathic absence of sentimentality made Malcolm an excellent CEO. Within five years, Rausing Oceanic grew successful under his watch. The company, which had previously specialized in undersea recovery and commercial diving support, expanded into custom shipbuilding, supplying littoral and amphibious watercraft for mercenary groups and small countries' militaries.

Malcolm became wealthier than even his father could have dreamed. He had no permanent address, but lived aboard his fleet of ships worldwide. The Aberdeen headquarters were merely symbolic and vestigial. Rausing's was a nomadic existence that suited him, living on the outlaw sea, free to sate his own appetites with no one watching.

In Sri Lanka, the Chinese were pumping money into infrastructure projects in exchange for long-term leases on deepwater ports, city property, and airports. It was a part of their "Belt and Road" initiative that would give them a strategic foothold in developing countries throughout Asia and Africa.

In Batticaloa, the small city on the east coast of Sri Lanka, a Chinese contractor had plans to develop a port for cargo vessels. It would require dredging a nearby lagoon, installing modern loading docks, and laying communications cables and pipework under the sea bed. Rausing Oceanic was hired for much of the underwater construction and commercial diving support. It would turn out to be the perfect cover for Malcolm Rausing's larger and more ambitious project.

The Deep Blue

Four miles south of Batticaloa, Sri Lanka.
Monday evening.

Just prior to entering Batticaloa, on the west side of the
A15 coast highway, sits a large lagoon that floods with
the high ocean tide. Every day, as they have for centuries,
enterprising local fishermen wait for the tide to ebb to
scout the shallow lagoon for mud crabs. These large
crustaceans are sold in the town markets up and down
the east coast, most often cooked into a deliciously spicy
curry. The dish was brought to Sri Lanka by Hindu
Tamils from India, but is distinctly non-denominational,
eaten by everyone but the most hardcore Buddhists, who
eschew eating any sort of sentient being.

As they drove across the lagoon bridge, Tusker
watched the fishermen poling the placid water for crabs.
Another time perhaps, this scene would seem serene.
It reminded him of road trips he'd taken back home, a
girlfriend sleeping off an early start while he enjoyed a
Lake Michigan summer sunrise. But he could only think
of Upali.

The town of Batticaloa lies roughly halfway down Sri
Lanka's eastern flank. In addition to its famous crabs, it

boasts a lighthouse built by the British in the early 1800s. The town's population has changed over its history, first Buddhist Sinhalese, then ethnic Tamils brought in by the British to work, and now, a large Muslim community. It is a small town, with a bustling high street jam packed with shops festooned with competing, mismatched signs and walls dripping with dark mildew. Women in hijabs carry umbrellas against the scorching equatorial sun and dodge the swaying buses that lurch past down the narrow streets.

Batticaloa has had a troubled history. It was at the heart of the eastern territory controlled by the rebel Liberation Tigers of Tamil Eelam during the civil war that ripped the country apart for decades. Then came the tsunami, and Batticaloa was ground zero. The low-lying town was consumed by a two-story wave that swept a mile inland, killing over 3,000 people and laying waste to anything in its path.

Road travel was exhausting in Sri Lanka. There was never a stretch of road where you could relax. The countless animals, motorbikes, and people on the narrow, winding roads meant it was constant slowing, stopping, and accelerating, all the while being pitched back and forth nauseatingly.

Ian managed to sleep in the front passenger seat for most of the six-hour drive, while Tusker brooded in the back, perched uncomfortably over the hot, noisy engine. *A full day wasted in this damn van*, he thought, looking out the dirty side window at the flashing scenery. When they stopped for a lunch of fish buns and tea at a roadside cafe back in Gampaha, Tusker didn't talk much, picking at his food and leaving his tea half drunk.

Back on the road, he turned over every possibility of how the *Taprobane* could have sunk. *We'll get out there and dive it as soon as possible*, he resolved to himself. *There will be clues. I'm an archaeologist after all.*

On the outskirts of Batticaloa, along an empty strip of sand and scrub pine, are several pockets of buildings that somehow survived the tsunami or were partially rebuilt. Stalks of rebar poke up from cement foundations, houses forever unfinished. It is out here, at the end of a long hard packed sand road, where you'll find the Deep Blue Resort and Diving School.

As the tired van bumped and lurched across the road, trailing a plume of dust, Tusker wondered why this man, Sebastian, would want to run a dive resort at this desolate dead end. He was starting to doubt they'd ever find it. Srivathnan had to stop every half mile or so to ask locals on bicycles where the place was, and it seemed like every one sent them in a different direction than the last. But finally, after passing under a canopy of low, thorny trees, Tusker saw the whitewashed wall of a building with the silhouette of a diver on it and the words *"Deep Blue Resort — We're the Wrecks-perts"* on it.

Tusker slid open the van's side door and shimmied out, bending over to stretch out his stiff back. Ian emerged sleepily, rubbing his eyes. The grounds of the resort were strangely silent, other than the ticking of the cooling engine and a chorus of buzzing cicadas somewhere in the trees. No one came to greet them and the place seemed deserted.

The Deep Blue was a series of single-story, white buildings with red tile roofs laid out almost like barracks, in a line with a stone path running in front of them. Each "hut" had a number on it, presumably the room numbers. Opposite the sleeping quarters was an open air dining area covered by a thatched roof and an enclosed kitchen at one end.

"Where's the welcoming committee?" Ian said. "I was expecting a pretty girl with an umbrella drink."

Tusker ignored him and crunched further up the path. At the far end, there was a larger building, a bit more industrial looking than the rest and painted dark green. He could hear the unmistakable muffled roar of a compressor emanating from within. He entered what was a sort of workshop, with scuba cylinders on the floor, two long workbenches with tools and hoses and parts of diving regulators and tank manifolds on them. The noise was louder. He moved into the back room, which was very warm and smelled of diesel. A shirtless Sri Lankan man with the stocky, powerful physique of a wrestler was hunched over a series of tanks with noise-protection earmuffs on his head. Tusker reached out and gently tapped the man on his bare shoulder. The man jumped and swung around with wide eyes.

"Sorry!" Tusker shouted over the din. This had to be Sebastian de Silva, the owner of the Deep Blue. From what Upali had told him months earlier, Tusker knew

Sebastian was a local diving legend, having been the first to locate the HMS *Hermes* wreck after Sri Lanka's civil war. Divers came from all over the world to stay at his out-of-the-way resort and dive with him.

Sebastian stepped away from the tanks and into the workshop room where it was quieter. He took off the earmuffs and wiped the sweat from his face with a greasy rag.

"You can put your diving gear in here," he said, bypassing any sort of greeting. He'd been expecting them. "With such short notice, I couldn't get my cleaner to prepare a new room for you. You can have your... friend's old room. Room 4." The MOCHA team had been staying at the Deep Blue for the past couple of days while out doing their sonar work and diving. Sebastian had known the MOCHA team well, and the strain of what had happened showed on his face.

"Thanks, that's not a problem," Tusker said. "We appreciate you putting us up." Sebastian ignored the comment and ducked back into the compressor room to disconnect the tank fill manifold. The compressor sang a higher pitch for a moment and then shut off. When Sebastian didn't emerge after a moment, Tusker stuck his head around the corner.

Sebastian was sliding a set of heavy twin cylinders across the shop floor. He seemed wholly intent on his work, as if he couldn't be bothered with niceties. If he felt bad about what had happened with the *Taprobane*, he didn't show it.

Tusker persisted. "Do you have any other guests?"

"Yes, two Russians who came to dive the *Hermes*, a
Swedish girl who's doing a nitrox course, and then
Roland. He's Dutch. Helps me out here, driving the boat,
dives occasionally."

"I see," replied Tusker. "We'll get ourselves settled then
and talk later." Sebastian gave a single nod and went back
to his work. Tusker walked back out to the van, where Ian
had unloaded most of their gear. Srivathnan was having
a smoke. He'd drive back to Galle that night. Tusker
couldn't imagine doing that trip in reverse again so soon,
but the quiet driver wanted to get home.

Tusker picked up his duffel bag and slung his buoyancy
harness over one shoulder. It was still damp from the
previous week's diving. *Was Sebastian running this whole
place by himself, with guests and dive courses to teach?* he
thought. As if in answer to his question, he heard an
engine approach up the dusty entrance road. It was
a battered blue Land Rover with a tire on its bonnet,
probably from the 1970s. It came to a stop, the engine
taking its time to shut off.

The driver's-side door opened and a young woman
stepped down. She flashed a brilliant white smile
at Tusker. She was Sri Lankan but not dressed in the
conservative saree of so many he'd seen on the streets
in Galle. Rather, she wore a pair of olive-colored cotton
shorts that showed off long sinewy thighs, with a khaki
ribbed tank top under an unbuttoned linen shirt. On her
wrist he noticed a beat-up Seiko diving watch hanging

loosely on a metal band. Her hair was shiny black, knotted in a braid that hung over her right shoulder. She had a pair of Ray-Ban aviators perched atop her head. He suddenly realized he was staring at her.

"Mister... Tusk?" she asked, grinning as if she knew the effect she had on him. Her accent had the lilt of most South Asians but Tusker detected something else, as if she'd grown up or studied elsewhere. Something to ask later perhaps. She lifted a cardboard box full of plastic water bottles off the passenger seat and kicked the door of the Land Rover shut with her heel.

"Yes, Julian Tusk," he finally replied, "but most people call me Tusker." How ridiculous, he thought.

She laughed a full, deep laugh, almost a man's laugh. "Why? Do you have big teeth, Mr. Tusk, or a big nose?"

"I'm just big," Tusker winked back. "And you are... ?"

"I'm Samanthi, Sebastian's daughter. I assume you've met Thathi, er... my father, already," she continued. "And Tusker, you can call me Sam." The smile again.

She remembered something and her face fell. "Dinesh from MOCHA told us you were arriving this afternoon. I'm really sorry about the circumstances. We really were fond of Upali and his team here. What a tragedy."

"Thanks, yeah," Tusker replied, following Sam as she carried the box to the Deep Blue's kitchen. "We came straightaway when we got the news. Any new

84

developments you've heard today?"

"No, I'm afraid not," Sam said, "Things progress slowly here in the best of times, Tusker. And this is not the best of times. The police are investigating what happened, but it's a bit tough when the crime scene—if it was a crime— is at the bottom of the ocean."

Ian joined them. "Has the navy offered to help? Surely they've got divers who could check things out."

"That would make sense," she answered, "but things here don't always make sense. There's a bit of a turf war between police and military, leftover grudge from the war, I guess."

"Maybe we can offer some assistance to the police," Tusker chimed in, "given our… unique skill set." He gestured to his dive gear.

"They've only just buoyed the site where the *Taprobane* went down," Sam said as she unpacked the water bottles and shoved them into a small refrigerator.

"Well, why don't we all chat about it after we get settled in our room," Ian said, his arms still full of dive gear from the van.

"Sure thing," Sam said. "I tried to tidy it as best I could. I put Upali's things in a duffel bag in the corner and laid some clean sheets on the table. Sorry, it's as far as I got."

"No problem, we'll manage," Tusker said. "So, I didn't

ask. You work here with Sebastian?"

Sam chuckled. "Sometimes I help out here. I'm a marine biologist by training, but this time of year, a lot of people come to dive the *Hermes*, and I dust off my old dive instructor certificate."

"Sorry, I didn't realize…" Tusker stumbled. He felt silly. Now her accent and style made sense. She'd probably studied in England or Australia.

Sam winked. "No worries. Most of my work is now in a lab or office, but every once in a while I like to get wet."

Tusker blushed. Ian broke in with an exaggerated cough, staring at Tusker.

"Alrighty, then," Tusker said then turned to leave and picked up his duffel. "We'll go get settled and catch up with you later. We're meeting with Dinesh from MOCHA this evening at the China Bay Club to see what he's found out."

"Sounds good," Sam said. "If you need to eat, we serve dinner anytime after seven."

Ian had turned and was walking up the path towards Room 4, his arms full of dive gear. He gave a side glance at Tusker and grinned. "Careful there, Romeo. She's clearly out of your league."

Tusker blushed. "Romance is the last thing on my mind," he said, as much to convince himself as Ian. He heaped his dive gear against the bare wall and caught sight of Upali's duffel. *Focus, Julian, focus,* he thought. "Right, so what's the plan then?"

"Let's hear what Dinesh knows. Then I'd like to get out and dive the *Taprobane* as soon as possible," Tusker said as he emptied his duffel on one of the beds. He wondered which one was Upali's.

As if reading his mind, Ian stepped back and huffed. "Man, it's hard to believe he's gone. I mean, just last week..." his voice trailed off.

The room was quiet and cool and dark. The ceiling fan ticked rhythmically above them.

"We'll find out what happened," Tusker said finally. "We owe it to Upali."

The Buddhist Power Army

Kandy, Sri Lanka.
Present day.

The Buddhist kingdom of Kandy was the last defiant holdout in Ceylon to foreign rule, fending off Portuguese and Dutch colonists for centuries, while the rest of Ceylon was subjugated. Finally, in 1815, the Kandyan royalty negotiated a truce with the British while maintaining a reputation for dignity and fierce resolve. While Colombo went on to become Sri Lanka's seat of government and commerce, the city of Kandy, and the mountainous interior that surrounds it, has long remained known as the hub of Sri Lankan Buddhism.

On the shores of picturesque Kandy Lake sits the Sri Dalada Maligawa, the temple of the sacred tooth relic, said to house a molar of the Buddha himself. It is a place of pilgrimage and ceremony for Buddhists and tourists alike. The annual Esala Perehara celebration sees elephant parades, music, and colorful dancers crowd the streets of Kandy in celebration of the tooth relic and Lord Buddha.

The city rises from the rectangular lake's banks, filling steep, verdant slopes with terraced gardens, old colonial houses, and humble neighborhoods. Orange-robed monks are a common sight, and the sound of Buddhist chanting mingles with the calls of tropical birds, often from dusk until dawn.

Its headlamps piercing a slashing rain, a black Toyota Land Cruiser crunched up the winding driveway, its mirrors brushing back branches of the banyan trees that tightly lined it. The big truck came to a stop in front of a low slung white building set in a clearing. Its wide eaves, built to fend off just such monsoon rains, were lined with carved wooden filigree—a row of swastikas, the ancient Buddhist symbol said to represent the footsteps of the Buddha. Colorful striped flags hung damp in the deluge. A loudspeaker echoed with the evening chants, lending an eerie reverence to the woodsmoke-tinged air.

Malcolm Rausing climbed out of the passenger seat and deployed a large black umbrella. He waved off Scholz, his driver, and walked towards the temple stairs, deftly stepping around the growing puddles. From the cool interior of the temple emerged a portly monk with a saffron robe slung over his shoulder. Rausing was struck by how smooth the man was: No eyebrows or body hair, head entirely shaved. He smiled and bowed, his palms together in the traditional Buddhist greeting.

"*Ayubowan,*" said Venerable Udugala Dhammasara, wishing Rausing a long and blessed life, and gestured for him to enter. "Please remove your shoes, Mr. Rausing." It was a high-pitched, soft voice that was incongruous with his bulk.

"*Ayubowan,*" Rausing said, half-heartedly pressing his

palms together. He slipped out of his shoes and ascended the stairs.

Rausing wondered just how old the Venerable Udugala Dhammasara was. His soft physique and lack of body hair lent him the look of an overgrown infant, yet the creases near his eyes and the way he labored to walk hinted at a man in his sixth or even seventh decade. As his name indicated, he was born in the town of Udugala and joined a monastery near Kandy as a young monk.

During the tumultuous 1980s, when the civil war divided Sri Lanka along ethnic and religious lines, splinter groups of Buddhist monks grew more and more aggressive, inciting riots and violence against the largely Hindu Tamil minority. One vocal leader, Venerable Pahathgoda Gnanatissa, could even be seen on the front lines of mobs marching through the streets of Colombo, encouraging his followers to burn Tamil businesses, and sometimes, their owners.

This crystalline resolve and singular focus resonated with Dhammasara and he became an acolyte of Gnanatissa, rising through the ranks of his newly formed *Bodu Bala Hamuda,* the Buddhist Power Army. After the civil war ended, a new government swept into power and vowed to bring those who incited violence to justice. Gnanatissa was jailed and Dhammasara took his place as the spiritual leader of the BBH. By this time, the BBH had a new target: the rising Muslim population in the east of Sri Lanka.

"How are you finding Batticaloa?" Dhammasara asked as they padded barefoot through the temple.

"It's hot," Rausing replied flatly. "And definitely different from Kandy or Colombo." He shot a knowing glance at the monk, who grunted in agreement. They walked together, passing a large chamber where a group of monks were sitting on the floor facing an elderly teacher.

At the end of a corridor, Dhammasara ushered Rausing into a small room. It was an office, with a dark wood desk, a few chairs and a framed portrait on the wall. The big monk took his chair behind the desk. He caught Rausing's gaze at the framed portrait. It was a sepia-tone photograph of a seated monk in a robe. The man wore a serious expression and, unlike the monks at this temple, had a full head of curly black hair.

"Anagarika Dharmapala," he said, answering the question he knew Rausing was about to ask. "He is the father of the Buddhist Protestant movement here in Sri Lanka and the spiritual ancestor of the *Bodu Bala Hamuda.*"

Rausing studied the old photo. The subject's eyes blazed white. Then he turned back to Dhammasara. He looked nothing like this historical forebear, but his eyes were equally on fire.

"Power and militancy do not seem compatible with most people's notion of Buddhism," Rausing said.

Dhammasara laughed. "You in the West have this image of Buddhists as lotus-eating, meditating pacifists, but there is a long tradition of our religion standing up for what is just and right, and of strong Buddhist warriors."

The monk rubbed his head thoughtfully. "It's not only the Muslims who can have their holy wars."

"You feel that Islam is not right and just?" Rausing countered. "I have no love for the Muslims, but then again, I'm not terribly fond of any religion."

Venerable Dhammasara shifted in his chair, which creaked ominously under his weight. "Buddhism is not a religion as you think of Islam or Christianity. It is more a way of life, a perspective on the world and a connection of one's spirit with nature. We just happen to follow the teachings of one particularly wise, or as we say, enlightened, man—the Buddha."

Rausing didn't react. In truth, he didn't care about the reasons Dhammasara had hired him and he regretted even being contrary.

Dhammasara continued. "Sri Lanka was historically a Buddhist land until the Europeans came and brought slaves from India with their own religions. Anagarika himself was the first to really stand up to this intrusion." He gestured to the scowling portrait. "The BBH is not against Muslims *per se*. But Islam has its holy lands in the Middle East. We Buddhists have ours here. The country is over 70 percent Buddhist as it is. It used to be higher." An enigmatic smile. "I'd like to return to that."

Rausing studied the monk's smooth face and dark eyes. "So, after you get rid of the Muslims, are the Christians next?"

"As Lord Buddha said, 'There is nothing mightier than patience'," Dhammasara replied.

"And no error greater than hatred," Rausing shot back.

The monk smiled. "You know your teachings, Mr. Rausing."

"Your motivation is of no concern to me. By the time you put your plan in place, I will be gone from this country."

"Well then, enough of the philosophical discussion," Dhammasara said. "Are you confident you can retrieve the weapon?"

"Certain." Rausing said. "We located it earlier this week but had a slight setback." He shifted uncomfortably, thinking of McElroy's failure and the *Taprobane*'s interference. Both problems had been eliminated; there was no need for this monk to know the details. "We'll be diving on the wreck later this week as soon as this weather system passes."

There was a flash and a loud crack of thunder. The monsoon rain was drumming on the roof above their heads.

"I'm glad to hear it," the monk rubbed his head and smiled. "Ramadan is in two weeks. We would like to be ready by then, for maximum effect."

"We'll make the exchange at our agreed-upon location. From there, you can do with it what you wish."

"As you like," Dhammasara said. "I will remain here and send some friends to collect it. The sea air doesn't agree with me."

Rausing hesitated, then asked, "What exactly are your plans with the weapon? It surely can't be used in its current state."

"That is none of your concern, Mr. Rausing." Dhammasara's tone grew colder. "We have friends with more experience who can help us with our needs." Then, he softened and said with a smile, "Just as you are helping us."

Dhammasara stood and gestured towards the door. The meeting was over. Rausing didn't rise. "We agreed on half of the money up front." He looked coldly up at the fat monk.

"Of course. It's already taken care of. I've had it loaded into your vehicle." Dhammasara gave a thin smile and pulled the door open. Rausing stood and followed him out.

"And the government will continue to not give us trouble?" Rausing stopped at the door. The rain had subsided and the air was heavy with moisture and the sound of insects, which had started their incessant nocturnal cacophony.

"The president is aware of our plans and has been fully supportive." The smile hung on Dhammasara's face, but his eyes were empty. Rausing looked away and nodded.

Venerable Dhammasara shuffled heavily through the quiet temple alongside Rausing, who was now eager to leave. "I trust the Chinese are paying you handsomely for your company's work in the new harbor?"

"Yes, they are a reliable and wealthy client," Rausing said, annoyed at the monk's prying question. He paused at the door to collect his shoes and fixed Dhammasara with his grey eyes. "Given the way the Chinese are buying up Sri Lanka, the Muslims won't be your only problem for long. But then, as you say, it's none of my concern." The slightest of smiles creased a corner of his cruel mouth. Venerable Dhammasara didn't react, but only pressed his palms together, then turned back into the temple.

As Rausing descended the steps outside, the Land Cruiser rolled up to collect him. Rausing slipped into the passenger seat and looked at his driver, Scholz, who nodded back. "All OK, sir?"

"Fine," Rausing replied, distractedly looking out the tinted glass at the dark scenery as Scholz pulled away. "Get me back to my ship."

The monk was a fanatic, a fool, and he despised him. But in a week it wouldn't matter. He would be far away from this forsaken island. The Land Cruiser passed Kandy Lake and headed onto the A9, back east to Batticaloa.

The China Bay Club

Trincomalee, Sri Lanka.
That evening.

The China Bay Club of Trincomalee can trace its origins back to 1882, when the British Navy bought the former home of a wealthy Dutch trader and turned it into a club for officers. The China Bay Club adhered to the protocols of the countless other clubs across Britain's vast empire: white-coated, dark-skinned servants waited on black-jacketed, white-skinned men of privilege who sipped gin and planned the course of history. The club, which was named for the crescent of water out its breezy windows, remained much the same up until the 1920s, when it opened up to a wider clientele, including civilians, wives, and the occasional mistress. By World War II, it became the center of the social scene in eastern Ceylon, peopled by international journalists, spies, and RAF pilots on leave from the nearby air base. After the war, and Ceylon's independence, locals were finally allowed entry and over the years the club has evolved into a thriving, diverse social scene, retaining its imperial charms but with more of an egalitarian buzz.

A flock of giant fruit bats flapped silently overhead as Tusker and Ian walked across the lawn. It was a warm night, with a sea breeze that coated everything in a salty sheen. Tusker wore a black linen shirt, open at the neck, and a pair of khaki trousers. He'd left his red Mount Gay cap behind for once, a sure sign he was dressing up. It was only the second time he'd worn long pants in Sri Lanka, but though the club had relaxed its jacket and tie policy, shorts were still frowned upon. Ian wore a pair of lime green pants and a dark blue polo shirt.

They were greeted warmly by a beautiful Southeast Asian woman at the reception, who asked if they had a reservation for dinner. "No, we'll just sit in the bar if that's OK, love," Ian said with his gap toothed grin. "By the way, do I detect a Vietnamese accent?" The woman blushed and nodded, gesturing to the room to her left, and the two men passed into the bar side of the club.

The bar ran the length of the room, and sunburned European tourists, well-heeled locals, handsome businessmen in blazers and long-legged women in short cocktail dresses were all bellied up to it. It was warm inside and Tusker pushed through to the wide verandah out back. A very drunk man and his date were just getting up from a table, and Tusker swooped in to claim it, sliding the collection of tonic water bottles and a heaped ashtray to one side.

A Sri Lankan waiter appeared immediately. He wore a stiffly starched white shirt with a black bowtie. Some things at the China Bay Club hadn't changed.

"We're waiting for a third, but I'll take a gin and tonic please, with plenty of ice, and a wedge of lime." The man nodded and looked at Ian, who ordered a lager and a bowl of spicy cashews.

The drinks arrived, glasses sweating in the humidity. The manicured lawn sloped away from the verandah into some coconut trees, the bay twinkling beyond. The ice in Tusker's glass was melting quickly, and he drank it fast and ordered another. He was tired from the day's long drive and thinking about Upali. Ian tried to make conversation.

"That Samanthi is a real cutie, eh?" He swigged from his bottle. Tusker didn't say anything. "Then again, you know what they say about dating the innkeeper's daughter." He laughed. Still nothing from Tusker. He tried a different tack.

"I wonder what Dinesh got out of the police. Did he call you?"

"Only to arrange a time to meet tonight," Tusker said, still looking out at the dark bay. He turned and banged his fist on the table so that the glass and tonic bottle clinked. Ian jumped. "It just can't have been an accident! Upali was as careful as they come, and boats don't just catch on fire."

"Yeah, but gas, electronics… and that Ranjith smoked like a chimney."

Tusker shook his head. Just then, a small, bald man with round glasses approached their table. Tusker's immediate impression was of Mahatma Gandhi, though instead of a robe, this man wore a striped button-down shirt and perfectly pressed grey trousers.

"Dinesh Ranasinghe." He smiled and extended a hand. Tusker stood up and pumped Dinesh's hand, then gestured for him to sit. The white-coated waiter returned.

"Just some cool water with lemon, please," Dinesh said, and the waiter disappeared. "Upali spoke very highly of you, Mr. Tusk," he said, turning to Tusker. "Said you were schoolmates."

"Yes, we were," Tusker replied. "Upali tends, er… tended to exaggerate though." He managed a smile. He was impatient with small talk. "What have you learned about the sinking?"

Dinesh shook his head and shifted in his chair. "The police seem to know very little and have no way of investigating what happened to the *Taprobane*. They don't have divers with that level of expertise and their relations with the navy are not good."

He took off his glasses and carefully wiped the lenses with a handkerchief. "I've offered MOCHA's assistance for crime scene photos. Our experience with sensitive archaeological sites would be of value, I'd have thought."

"But?" Ian chimed in.

"But this police captain, Gooneratne, was not interested," Dinesh said. "They're relying solely on eyewitnesses, which is slim evidence indeed, seeing as the boat was anchored offshore and it was 7:00 in the morning."

"Well, I'd like to go speak with this policeman myself tomorrow. Maybe we can wear him down and at least be allowed to produce some photos and evidence and…" he hesitated, "recover any bodies."

Just then, a tall man strode up silently to their table and stood over Dinesh.

"Sorry to interrupt," he said, in an accent that was hard to place. Scottish? Danish?

"You are Dinesh Ranasinghe from the Ministry of Culture, Heritage and Archaeology, correct?" The man was very pale and, despite the heat, wore a thin navy turtleneck and cream-colored linen trousers. He was not sweating, from what Tusker could see, and had a beard and silvery hair pulled tightly back in a ponytail, showing a scar on his forehead.

Dinesh stood up. He was a full head shorter than this man. "Yes, I am he," he replied, extending his hand. "And you are…?"

"Rausing, Malcolm Rausing," the man said. "I wanted to express my condolences about your colleagues. What an awful business."

Dinesh was taken aback. "Ah, thank you, Mr. Rausing." he managed. "How did you know I worked for MOCHA?"

Rausing smiled and ignored the question. He turned to Tusker. "And your friends?"

"This is Mr. Julian Tusk and Ian Walsh," Dinesh introduced them. "They were friends of one of the men who was on the *Taprobane*."

"As I said, awful business," Rausing said, shaking his head while eyeing Tusker. "I own the *Depth Charge*, the ship doing some work in the new harbor. If there's anything we can do to help..."

Tusker didn't like the man and was impatient to get back to the conversation with Dinesh. "Thank you, Mr. Rausing. We're working with the police to find out what happened to the *Taprobane*."

"Of course, of course," Rausing nodded vigorously. "But my offer stands. I have a crew of accomplished divers ready to help."

"Thank you very much," Dinesh chimed in, sensing the tension between Rausing and Tusker. "Mr. Tusk and Mr. Walsh are actually expert divers as well."

"Is that so?" Tusker thought he saw the shadow of surprise cross Rausing's face. "Well, do be careful out here. The currents in the east can be tricky, and the sea floor gets deep rather quickly."

"I thought your crew was in the harbor," Ian said. Rausing's eyes blazed at him, then he eased into a smile.

"We are, but have managed to take the odd day off for some offshore diving fun," he said. "Well, I won't keep you from your drinks. It was nice to meet you, gentlemen." He turned to go, then paused. "And do give my regards to Captain Gooneratne." Then he was gone. Tusker watched the tall figure stride across the crowded verandah and into the darkness.

A Police Matter

Batticaloa, Sri Lanka.
The next day.

"It was an explosion," Captain Sunil Gooneratne said, blowing ripples across the surface of his cup of tea. "The fishermen said it went up like fireworks. Sank fairly quickly too."

Tusker sat across the worn metal desk and mopped the sweat from the back of his neck. He and Ian had endured an hour in the lobby of the Batticaloa police station, waving away flies with a small queue of locals who were waiting to file some complaint or other.

"Did any debris wash ashore? Any sense of how it happened?" Tusker already didn't like the chubby captain and his indifference. He controlled his annoyance, knowing that to show exasperation would only make things worse.

"We collected a couple of life jackets and a wetsuit. Empty of course, but nothing else." The captain smiled, as if at a joke. "I'm sure with all those scuba tanks and electronics on board, that boat was a floating bomb."

Tusker leaned forward in his chair, a blood vessel in his neck pulsing.

Ian put a hand on Tusker's arm and interjected. "Have you been able to examine the wreck yet? Surely that would help explain how it exploded."

"Mr. Walsh, we are a busy police force here in Batticaloa and don't have the time or resources to be out scuba diving." He made it sound like it was a holiday snorkel.

"You see, here in the East, we are understaffed and have other serious matters. Surely you know, we have all these Muslims here, not like in Galle or Colombo..." He gave a knowing look at Ian and Tusker, as if they would sympathize.

After the Easter bombings, the country had descended into the same paranoid divisions that plagued Europe and the West, and there was tension between the Buddhist majority Sinhalese and the Muslim population, which was concentrated in the cities of the east coast.

Ian smiled back, ignoring Gooneratne's thinly veiled bigotry. "What about the navy? Or the coast guard? Wouldn't this fall into their jurisdiction to investigate? It seems awfully suspicious that a boat would just explode."

"This is a police matter, Mr. Walsh," he replied. "Anyway, I told all of this already to your friend, this Dinesh from Colombo." He stood up as if to signal their time was up. "We'll be completing our investigation, interviewing witnesses, and will release a report when we finish."

The police captain walked around his desk and
extended his hand. "I know things in England and
America work differently, but here in Sri Lanka, we
have our own process. Now, thank you for your concern
and your time. I have a number of other citizens who
require my attention."

Outside, Tusker was silent — fuming. "Guess it's time to
go check out the *Taprobane*," Ian said.

"Yes," Tusker said. "Let's do that, now."

Sebastian was nowhere to be found when they returned
to the Deep Blue. Tusker walked past the workshop to the
small swimming pool used for dive training, its surface
matted with yellow leaves and dead bugs. At one end,
a girl was splayed out on a towel in a bikini, her arm
shielding her face from the sun. She was talking to an
older man who squatted in the shade, smoking a cigarette.
They both looked up at Tusker.

"Hello." The girl sat up and squinted "You must be Julian."

"Tusker," he corrected her. "Have you seen Sebastian?"

She ignored his question. "I'm Anja." She smiled a
brilliant white smile and peered over the top of large
dark glasses, assessing him. Her accent was musical,
Scandinavian. The Swedish girl Sebastian had told them
about, no doubt. She was deeply tanned and beautiful,
with the lithe body of an athlete. Cross-country skier,
Tusker let himself muse.

The man came out of the shadow of the tree. He was older, maybe 50, with leathery skin and pale blue eyes. He wore surf trunks and a stained t-shirt, faded from red to a sort of pink, with the logo of a Caribbean diving resort on it. He walked over to Tusker and held out his hand. "Roland Van der Schyff. I'm from the Netherlands." His smile was yellow and his voice had the tortured hoarseness of a regular smoker.

"Nice to meet you both," Tusker said, finding his manners despite his impatience. "I'm looking for Sebastian. Hoping to get out diving this afternoon."

"Sebastian is out with the Russkies," Roland replied. "Diving the *Hermes*."

"Is there a second boat?" Tusker asked.

"I could take you out. I'm sort of an unofficial second mate around here. You know, fill tanks, fix boat motors, that sort of thing. Where do you want to dive?"

"Just outside the lagoon. The wreck of the *Taprobane*."

"Is that a good idea, Cap'n? I mean, isn't that a police matter?" Roland fidgeted with a damp cigarette.

"I just spoke with the police, and they're not equipped to investigate the sinking." Tusker said, matter-of-factly. *It's not really a lie.*

"Well, if you think so, Cap'n, I can run you out there. Drops off deep just there, I think. You'll want double

106

tanks. Could run into a little decompression time."

"Great," Tusker said, already turning to go, "I'll meet you in the shop for some tanks."

"See you later, Tusker," Anja called to him. Tusker pivoted and gave a wave. Another time, he'd have gotten to know her. But he was preoccupied and in no mood for the coy parry and thrust of seduction.

Ian was in their room, making a heap of dive gear on the floor. "Any luck?" he said to Tusker.

"Yeah, the Dutch guy is going to take us out. We'll dive doubles."

"I figured this was deco territory. Everything worth diving over here is deep. Sorry, that didn't come out right." Ian said, sheepishly.

An hour later, they were motoring out of the lagoon in a small fiberglass skiff loaded with gear. There was no canopy against the sun. The sea was flat calm and shimmered as if covered with a film of oil. They had no trouble spotting the makeshift buoy the police had placed to mark the location where the *Taprobane* had sunk. It consisted of no more than a cinder block dropped over the side, 200 feet of nylon rope, and a plastic bottle. As Roland slowed the boat, Tusker looked around and felt a spasm of sadness. He thought back to that last text message from Upali. He had been excited about finding a new wreck, the dream of any marine archaeologist. He never could have imagined ending like this, Tusker was sure of it.

"I can't really tie off to this buoy, but there's not much current," Roland said. "I'll just keep the boat around while you guys are under. Don't worry, I'll be here when you come back." The yellow smile.

Tusker nodded back. The charts showed the depth at around 180 feet, well beyond recreational limits and necessitating some decompression before they could surface. A 20-minute dive would require 50 minutes of decompression: hanging on the buoy line in stages as they slowly ascended, allowing their bodies to respirate the excess nitrogen that had been forced into their blood vessels and tissues. Taking into account time and greater air consumption at depth, Ian and Tusker both wore twin 80–cubic foot cylinders of air, with two regulators for redundancy, just in case.

Lifting that gear up to the tiny boat's gunwales was clumsy, heavy work. Sitting on opposite sides of the boat, Tusker and Ian made eye contact and Roland gave a countdown. "3, 2, 1, go!" Tusker and Ian backrolled simultaneously over the side into the water and immediately descended into the indigo blue water.

Sunken Crime Scene

Bay of Bengal, one mile offshore of Batticaloa.
The same day.

Tusker could see the *Taprobane*'s white foredeck below
as soon as he began descending, as if she was still afloat
and he was hang gliding above her. The ship lay upright
on the sea floor. At first, she showed no signs of damage,
and Tusker found himself thinking that maybe there
was no explosion. Could it have just sank, and the crew
swam ashore? It wasn't that far offshore. *It was all just a
misunderstanding.*

Then he saw the body.

It was Suresh, the sonar expert. Tusker had met him back
in Galle when they were surveying the harbor. Tusker
remembered giving him a hard time for being afraid of
the water, threatening to push him overboard if he didn't
behave. His body was pressed up against the inside of the
cabin window, pinned by the buoyancy of his orange life
jacket, which he always dutifully donned before leaving
the dock. Tusker looked at Ian and could tell he'd seen
the same thing.

Tusker settled on the sand bottom where the *Taprobane*

rested and checked his depth gauge. 187 feet. He briefly watched the march of the Aquastar's seconds hand tick tick tick around the dial. Its steady precision calmed him. Ian nudged him with a quizzical look. *Snap out of it, man.* At this depth, the nitrogen in the air they were breathing had a narcotic effect. It affected people differently. Some got paranoid, others panicked, but for Tusker, it caused time to slow down. On some deep dives he'd become obsessed in minutiae, staring at the nibbling of a fish or the seconds hand of his watch in what afterwards felt like a timeless fugue state.

A newly sunken 46-foot wreck is easier to explore than a larger, older one. While Tusker explored the torn rear dive deck and cabin, Ian swam down the length of its white hull and around behind the transom, which had been customized by MOCHA to allow easier entry for divers climbing the ladder. Then he saw the gaping wound in the boat's port-side hull. The white aluminum was now black and twisted. He could see into the engine compartment through the ragged gash. He banged his tank to get Tusker's attention.

Tusker swam down to Ian and saw the maw in the hull. He reached into the pocket on his harness belt and took out a measuring tape. He ran it along the hole in the hull and made note of it on a waterproof slate strapped to his wrist. He pulled the knife from its sheath on his lower leg and prised off a small flapping piece of the torn steel hull. He swam a few feet away to take another look. Tusker thought for a moment. *This wasn't the result of any scuba tank exploding.* The pattern of damage reminded him of sunken warships he'd surveyed that had been hit by torpedoes or collided with mines.

Ian was below, scouring the sea floor for clues. It occurred to Tusker that Ian was spending longer at greater depth than he was. *He can take care of himself.*

Tusker swam inside the boat's cabin and began carefully pulling debris out of the forward hold, looking for anything at all that might provide answers. It was all ropes, cushions, life jackets, and a jumble of tools and equipment. Suresh's body was still trapped against the window. There was no way to do a body recovery with Roland and that small skiff. They would have to have Captain Gooneratne send out a police boat and then float Suresh's body, and any others they found, to the surface with lift bags. It was grim business.

Where were the other bodies? Probably thrown overboard by the explosion, Tusker thought. Or maybe they jumped off when the *Taprobane* started to sink. They'd either be on the sea floor somewhere or would wash up on a beach down south in a few days.

The ROV was lying a few yards off of the wrecked boat, looking ready for action. Could it be salvaged and returned to MOCHA? Tusker made note of that for later. They'd come back tomorrow with Sebastian and do a more thorough survey, raise the ROV and maybe Suresh's body.

He checked his pressure gauge. He'd breathed close to half his air supply, well over the recommended "rule of thirds," which kept one-third for the ascent and one-third for a safety reserve. The Aquastar indicated they'd been down for 22 minutes. On his right wrist, Tusker checked his Sherwood dive computer. It was a few years old, and he never wore it for the shallow excavation work, but here in deep water it was valuable for calculating his decompression stops on the way up. It was flashing 41 minutes of deco time. They had to start their ascent now.

Tusker shouted through his mouthpiece to Ian and tapped him on the leg. Ian swiveled around. Tusker tapped his wrist and then made the "thumbs up" sign— time to ascend. Ian nodded and they both gave a few kicks to start their ascent. They rose slowly, careful to vent their buoyancy harnesses to prevent a runaway ascent, following the yellow line of the buoy. At 90 feet, Tusker paused, the Sherwood beeping at him, indicating the first deep stop. The nitrogen narcosis fog lifted.

Tusker looked down. The *Taprobane* was still clearly visible, almost a hundred feet below. Above him, he could see the outline of the skiff drifting a ways off of the buoy.

The Sherwood beeped again. Up to 80 feet for one minute and 70 for another. Then he crept up the line: 60 feet for two minutes, 50 feet for three minutes, 40 for four. After a few more short stops, Tusker and Ian paused at 15 feet for 20 minutes. The water was warm here and bright. The surface was tantalizingly close, but to cut short decompression now would risk paralysis or even death.

Finally the Sherwood beeped an "All Clear" and Tusker and Ian surfaced. The skiff was 30 feet away. Roland was sunning himself, talking on a cell phone to someone. At Tusker's shout, Roland quickly put the phone down and pulled the outboard to life. "Sorry, fellas, didn't see you come up!"

They handed their weight belts and dive gear up to Roland and heaved themselves over the gunwales into the boat. Roland swung the skiff around in a dramatic arc and gunned it. The hull banged across the swells towards the lagoon. "Find anything down there?" he shouted.

Tusker didn't feel like sharing details. "Well, it was no accident, I can tell that much." Roland just grinned, his yellow teeth clamped around a cigarette.

Back at the Deep Blue, the other skiff was pulled up on the shore. Sebastian and the Russians were back. Tusker jumped off the bow and turned to help Ian with the dive gear.

"I'm not feeling great, mate," Ian said weakly. He crouched next to the boat then suddenly lurched forward and fell to the sand. He vomited violently.

"Ian!" Tusker yelled. He knew the signs: the nitrogen Ian had inhaled under pressure had started to expand in his blood vessels and his joints. His crippled posture and extreme pain were what gave decompression sickness its nickname: "the bends."

Gitche Gumee

Four miles south of Batticaloa, Sri Lanka.
Later that night.

It was late when the aptly named Tata Nano taxi buzzed
off, leaving Tusker in a cloud of oily two-stroke exhaust
back at the Deep Blue. Ian was in the hyperbaric chamber
at the Trincomalee naval base up the coast and would stay
there for the next few days. For a while there, Tusker had
worried he wasn't going to make it. Roland had helped
him get a taxi from the resort for the drive up the A15.
Ian was curled in a spasmodic husk of pain in the back
seat the whole way, sucking on the emergency oxygen kit
Tusker had found in Sebastian's workshop. Then it ran
dry. The doctor had said he'd need at least four days in
the chamber while his body was brought back down to a
simulated depth and then decompressed slowly. If he was
lucky, Ian might regain use of his legs one day.

Tusker was supposed to be getting on a plane back to the
U.S. soon. His visiting fellowship in Sri Lanka was set to
end, and a new semester of teaching back at Michigan
Tech would be starting in a couple months. He could
imagine the mail that had piled up back at the post
office in Copper Harbor. Then there was the fieldwork
in Jamaica next winter to start preparing for. But that all

seemed so distant now. He was only thinking one day at a time, for the first time in years.

The light was on in the dining area, and though he didn't feel like socializing, Tusker ducked under the thatched roof. Sebastian was sitting alone at a table, eating a plate of rice and curry with his fingers. He looked tired but beckoned Tusker to sit down. "Eat something? You must be very hungry." He called out in Sinhala and the cook, a rail-thin old man in a sarong and dirty button-up shirt, appeared out of the kitchen. "You want chicken? Fish?" Sebastian asked Tusker.

"Fish." Tusker didn't feel like eating, but he couldn't remember the last meal he'd had.

"*Malu*," Sebastian said, and the old man nodded and disappeared again. The smell and sound of frying food emanated from the kitchen.

"Roland told me what happened," Sebastian said. "Dr. Senanayake is a good doctor. Your friend is in good hands."

"I think he was deeper than me for most of the dive. I should have alerted him to it."

"Well, everyone reacts differently, and a lot can depend on diet, dehydration, how much sleep he had, if he was stressed."

Tusker nodded. Sebastian was trying to be helpful, but his words felt empty. Tusker had seen the effects of decompression sickness before. Watching Ian writhing in the back of the taxi brought to the surface raw emotion. With Upali's death, it was almost too much to bear. And yet, what was pushing foremost in his mind was that hole in the *Taprobane*.

"Did Upali mention anything about their work? Anything strange?"

Sebastian finished chewing while he thought. "He was pretty excited two nights ago by what they found. Thought it was the *Vampire*." He took a swig from a bottle of ginger beer. "But he did say they had found something peculiar in the wreck. Didn't say what but said he needed to make a trip up to Trincomalee... the navy base, as a matter of fact, to ask them about it. That was the morning they went out to get more video footage." He looked down at his food.

The cook came out with a steaming plate heaped with white samba rice smothered in chunks of a meaty fish with a yellow gravy. It smelled delicious.

"Would you like a fork?" Sebastian asked him.

"No, I've gotten pretty good with my fingers." Tusker managed a weak smile. "Though I do eat with my left hand. I know that's a no-no."

Sebastian smiled and wobbled his head. "As you wish."

"Did Upali show you any footage from the ROV?" Tusker said as he dipped his fingers, knuckle deep, into the curry.

It was hot.

"He did show me some screen grabs. It sure looks like a warship, guns and all." Sebastian replied. "Oh, he did mention one more thing that seemed odd," Sebastian said as he rinsed the fingers of his right hand in a small bowl of water and lime. "The day they found the wreck, there was this big commercial diving ship anchored right over the spot. He asked if I knew anything about it or its owner. I said I didn't. The crew seems to keep to themselves and stay onboard, even when they're docked in Batticaloa, working on that harbor project."

Tusker was wolfing down his curry, shoveling it inexpertly into his mouth from the plate. He stopped chewing. "What is the ship's name?"

"The DSV *Depth Charge,*" Sebastian said.

"Rausing," Tusker said and slid back his chair. He recalled the silver-haired man at the China Bay Club who'd taken such interest in the *Taprobane.*

"Yes, I think he's the owner," Sebastian said absent-mindedly. He had opened a laptop and was scrolling through GoPro video footage from that day's diving on the *Hermes* with the Russians.

"I'd like to dive the *Taprobane* again tomorrow," Tusker said. "Can you take me out? Maybe join me for the dive? I'd love to get your take on what I found this morning."

"I'm afraid I'm back on the *Hermes* again tomorrow,"

Sebastian said. "But Samanthi will be here and I'm sure she could go along."

"OK, sounds good," said Tusker. "I'll find her in the morning. Good night, Sebastian."

He got up and walked out of the dining area's island of light and into the dark night. The path was hard to see and he stumbled. Something scurried away under his feet. He found Room 4, put the key in the lock, went in and shut the door behind him.

Across from Room 4, in the dark beneath the low-hanging branch of an almond tree, the orange tip of a cigarette sizzled to life and then dimmed.

Tusker flipped on the light and did his usual scan of the floor and walls for insects and reptiles. Nothing. He kicked off his cheap rubber slippers and switched on the ceiling fan. The room was still and hot, but he dared not open the windows, lest a swarm of malarial mosquitoes come for his moist, pale skin. He sat on the edge of the bed and rubbed his face. It was close to midnight. He was exhausted, but something wouldn't let him sleep just yet.

In the corner of the room, Upali's belongings were neatly arranged. He padded over and gingerly sorted through them. It seemed almost sacrilege. A large black cockroach flitted out from beneath the duffel bag, making straight for the bathroom door. Tusker jumped back, swore, and nearly stomped on it before realizing he was barefoot. "You live another day," he called after it.

He picked up Upali's leather and canvas shoulder bag, the faded one Tusker had given him many years ago as a birthday gift. "It'll help you fit in better here," Tusker had joked with him. Upali had carried it throughout their college days in Michigan. A wave of sadness passed through Tusker as he opened it.

Inside was a notebook and laptop computer, along with an energy bar and a crumpled lightweight rain jacket. He pulled out the notebook and thumbed its pages, which were rippled and smeared from moisture. He found the last page. In Upali's hurried, sloppy penmanship was simply a set of GPS coordinates and a word, underlined: "Helmet?"

Had they found a military helmet? If it was a navy vessel, this wouldn't be unusual. So why had he questioned it?

Tusker set aside the notebook and pulled out the laptop, an old MacBook covered in decals. He opened it and booted it up. It was locked. Tusker cursed. What was Upali's password? He tried to remember if he'd ever shared it. He tried a few configurations of "UpaliK," to no avail. Then variations of "MOCHA," with no luck. *What was Upali's mother's name? His cat?*

Then something came to mind. Back at Michigan Tech, he and Upali'd taken a course in deepwater shipwreck archaeology. The most famous wreck in the Great Lakes was the *Edmund Fitzgerald*, a 700-foot-long freighter that sank in a storm in 1975. It was a case study in how to survey a deep wreck, since the ship lay in over 500 feet of water in Lake Superior. "The legend lives on, from the Chippewa on down, of the big lake they call Gitche Gumee." The Lightfoot song. They'd just been singing last week in Galle. It was worth a try.

Tusker typed "gitchegumee." The computer screen opened up. There was a series of folders on the computer's desktop named for dates. He chose the last one and opened it. It was a series of video files with long, nonsensical names. He methodically began double-clicking on each one, watching the harsh, contrasty footage from what was obviously the ROV. It showed the *Vampire*. There was the bow railing; there was a nine-inch cannon. The crumpled superstructure. Incredible. But no clues.

Tusker yawned and looked at his watch. It was 1:30. He opened the last video. The ROV was approaching a hatch in the hull of the wreck. It went in, its landing skid barely brushing the edge of the opening. Damn, Suresh was good. The bright lights pierced the darkness inside the ship, and then, there it was. Tusker's skin went cold.

He picked up the notebook again. Now it made sense. The helmet.

Exotic Gas

Four miles south of Batticaloa, Sri Lanka.
The next day.

"That's suicide!" Sebastian shouted over the noise of
the compressor. "I'm sorry, but we aren't equipped
to support a dive that deep. You'd need safety divers,
bailout bottles, and a bigger boat for all those cylinders!"
He switched off the compressor and turned to face Tusker.
"You've already put one diver in the chamber this week.
More than that starts to look bad for business!"

Tusker stood with his hands in his pockets. He'd
anticipated this reaction when he told Sebastian he
wanted to dive the *Vampire* instead of the *Taprobane*.
"Look, I appreciate your concern and the seriousness
of doing a dive like this. I've done it before, in far more
dangerous conditions." Back in '08, Tusker led an
expedition to dive the wreck of the *Carl D. Bradley*, to
commemorate the fiftieth anniversary of that freighter's
sinking. It had gone down in 330 feet of water in Lake
Michigan, taking all but one of its 30 crew members with
her. Not that it mattered. Sebastian didn't ask.

Sebastian brushed past Tusker. "Well, you're not going out
on my boat and I'm not letting my daughter go with you."

"OK, fine," Tusker called back and followed Sebastian out of the workshop. "We'll stick to the *Taprobane*. I assume Roland can take us again?"

Sebastian stared warily for a moment then nodded. "Yes. He's already loading the boat. Samanthi will be here at 9:00."

Tusker went back into the workshop and gathered up his dive gear, remembering to give his booties a good shake. He'd go down on the *Vampire*. After Sebastian left with the Russians in the morning, he'd load up the extra tanks. Roland surely wouldn't care which wreck they dove. And Sam could be a safety diver. He wouldn't expect her to take the same risk as him, but he could use her help during the long deco stops, ferrying extra bottles down to him.

Hanging next to his own kit was Ian's, still damp from yesterday's diving. Tusker thought of his friend, lying up in Trinco in the hyperbaric chamber.

Was he being reckless? Would it be smarter to go plead with the police or the navy to investigate? He could show them the ROV footage and tell them about the *Taprobane*.

No. That could take days, and imagine looking at the police captain's face again; besides, the police and the navy had a turf war. The *Vampire*. He owed it to Upali, and now to Ian, to sort this out himself.

He heard the crunch of a vehicle on the gravel driveway behind the workshop. It was the old blue Land Rover.

Sam stepped out. The driver's door didn't shut the first time and she gave it a hard slam.

"British engineering at its finest, eh?" Tusker laughed. Sam smiled back behind her aviators.

She opened the tailgate. In the back was a faded mesh duffle full of diving gear. He walked over to give her a hand. "Thathi told me about Ian. That's rough. We've had a handful of guys get slightly bent on the *Hermes*, but it sounds like he's got it bad." She shouldered the duffel and handed a pair of fins to Tusker.

"We dove a similar profile, but he really got hit hard," Tusker said. He mentally debated how to tell her he was going to dive the *Vampire*.

"Well, let's be careful today, yeah?" Sam said. She had on a pair of cutoff denim jeans and a faded t-shirt from the University of New South Wales. He could see the tied strap of a bikini top poking out of the neckline.

They walked through the workshop, where Tusker picked up his gear, then down the sandy path through the screw pine to the beach where the skiff was pulled up. There, they heaped the gear into the boat and turned back. Tusker was already sweating profusely. *Stay hydrated*, he told himself, remembering that one of the contributing factors of decompression sickness is dehydration.

"I assume we're diving air at the bottom and 50 percent nitrox for deco?" Sam asked as they walked back to the workshop.

"I'm thinking of breathing something a little more...
exotic," Tusker said.

"Why?" Sam shot back. "This wreck is what, 55, 60 meters?"

"I might want to explore something a little deeper, and
a helium blend might be a nice cushion," Tusker said
casually. He was going to have to tell her. She stopped
walking and put her hands on her hips.

"Look, man, I'm up for anything, but you have to give me
a little more detail. None of this cowboy diving shit." Her
accent got more clipped, and the Australian came through.

Tusker lowered his voice and glanced around for
Sebastian. He caught sight of him talking to the Russians
in the dining area. "Mind if we go back to my room?"

"Well, you don't waste time, do you?" She smirked. "I
said I was up for anything, but we only just met."

Tusker laughed. "I just want to show you something.
Then you can decide what you're up for."

They walked back to Room 4 and slipped in, hoping
Sebastian wouldn't see them. Tusker felt like a guilty
teenager. The room was still dark and cool, and he didn't
switch on the light. He pulled out Upali's laptop, and
Sam sat down next to him on the bed and leaned in close
to the screen. Her hair brushed his arm. She smelled of
sandalwood.

Tusker showed her the video clips from the *Vampire*, from the very beginning right up to the yellow diving helmet. She drew in her breath when it came onto the screen, then sat back and looked at him.

"See, this is why I need to get down there," he said. "Something is not right here."

The last clip was paused showing the yellow helmet. Sam pointed at the corner of the screen, where the ROV's digital statistics were overlaid. "There's a reason whoever was down there had a diving helmet. 100 meters is saturation diving territory."

"Well, it looks like that didn't go so well for them, doesn't it?" He tapped the helmet on the screen. "I know right where to look. If I can just get a few more clips on a GoPro, I'll have definitive proof to take to the police, or the navy. I'm thinking ten minutes on the bottom, no more."

Sam leaned back on the bed, resting on her elbows. "What's the deco time for a dive that deep for that long?"

"Just shy of three hours. We can take sling bottles of nitrox for deco and hang a couple of 100 percent O_2 tanks from the skiff at ten feet. This all assumes Roland is up for it." He suddenly realized he'd included her in this plan. "That is, only if you're comfortable with it. You could stay shallower and be my safety diver..."

"I'm game," she interrupted. "I've been to 75 meters on a wreck in Aussie. What is that in old currency... 230 feet?

We dove trimix for that. If we stick to a plan and keep an eye on each other, we can do this."

Tusker had the sudden urge to lean over and kiss her hard on the mouth. Something about the impending risk of the dive and her willingness to go along with it sent a palpable charge fizzing through the dark room. Did she sense it too? Sam sat up quickly and got to her feet. "Alright, let's see what Thathi's got for helium in the shop. He usually keeps some to blend for the rebreather divers."

"Oh, there's one more thing," Tusker said before she got to the door. "Your father said he won't allow this and doesn't want you to go. I told him we're sticking to the *Taprobane*."

She grinned mischievously. "This feels like school days. I used to meet this guy…" She paused. "Oh, never mind. I won't tell him if you don't." She walked out and left the door open.

Two hours later, they were motoring out of the lagoon. The skiff was badly overloaded with tanks and Roland had to carefully maneuver it through the shallows. The midday heat was already bringing the steady offshore breeze, and outside the shelter of the lagoon, swells were kicking up, sending spray into the boat.

"It's going to be harder to find that buoy in these waves," Roland shouted above the noise of the under-matched outboard.

Tusker looked at Sam, then back to Roland. "We're

going somewhere different today, if you don't mind," he shouted. "It's only a bit further north. I've got the GPS coordinates. I'll tell you when we're close."

Roland frowned but didn't reply. Tusker pulled out a small handheld GPS unit. It was an old Garmin he'd used since grad school to mark anomaly sites during sonar surveys. He pushed his sunglasses up on the brim of his cap and squinted at the tiny screen. Without lifting his head, he gestured ahead and to the right, guiding Roland. The skiff bounced over the swells, the motor straining.

"All right, slow down!" Tusker called out. Roland throttled back the little Yamaha outboard. "40 meters… 30… OK, Sam, get the anchor ready."

Sam shimmied to the bow of the skiff and pulled a small grapple from the pile of life jackets and rope. She perched herself on the gunwale, waiting for Tusker's command. "I hope there's enough line!" She shouted over her shoulder.

Tusker hadn't thought of that."OK, let's try here. Drop the anchor!"

Sam hurled the anchor over the side and paid out the rope, making sure it didn't foul on the chaos of gear that clogged the bottom of the boat. The rope snaked out for what seemed like minutes. Finally it went slack.

"OK, Roland, let's slowly motor forward to see if we're hooked."

Roland revved the motor and the skiff moved forward.

Sam held the rope with both hands and pulled on it. It went tight. "I think we're good!" she called out.

Nice work, Upali, Tusker thought. *Dead on, first try.* His coordinates were perfect. In the bow of the skiff, Tusker noticed that there was no spare line coiled. They'd used it all.

"What's this spot?" Roland asked in the silence after he switched off the motor.

"We want to check out this new wreck Upali thought he found," Tusker replied as he stripped off his T-shirt.

"Huh, that Aussie warship he was on about?" Roland asked, fishing for his cigarette pack.

"We'll find out." Tusker smiled cagily. Shipwreck hunters were a secretive bunch, their obsession with privacy only exceeded by the CIA and maybe Swiss banks. Part of it came from the early days of claiming salvage rights to whatever booty could be plundered from a wreck, but even weekend trollers on the Great Lakes were tight lipped about their sonar grids. Tusker didn't know Roland very well, nor did he trust him all that much. But today he'd have to, since he and Sam would be hanging underneath his boat for the whole afternoon.

"This is gonna be a deep one, Roland," he conceded a bit, to gain the Dutchman's confidence. "We may be down there a while. Maybe three, three and a half hours."

Roland smiled, his tobacco-stained teeth flashing. "Roger

that, Cap'n. Cell signal is good enough out here for me to stream some porn. Should keep me occupied." He shot a leering glance at Sam, who'd stripped down to her bikini and was pulling on a wetsuit. "Just to kill some time."

She ignored him and shimmied halfway into a black five-millimeter suit. Tusker watched her from the corner of his eye while he pulled on his own wetsuit. Her shoulders were deep brown and tight with muscle, and as she reached up to tie her hair back, he saw her flat stomach. Her navel had a silver ring through it.

He turned to Roland, who winked. Tusker frowned back at him. "Just don't fall asleep and let the anchor come unhooked. And if you can, hang some O_2 bottles over the side for our last deco stop."

"Sure thing, Cap'n." He blew out a stream of smoke and leaned back against the gunwale.

Tusker took off his Mount Gay Rum cap and tossed it in the bottom of the skiff. "Don't lose my cap, Roland."

The Dutchman nodded back. "I'll keep it safe."

He and Sam busied themselves kitting up, a heavy process made all the more difficult by the cramped quarters of the tiny skiff. The dozen tanks were piled on top of each other, and they had to awkwardly walk over them to reach their gear. Roland made no effort to help.

Finally, Sam and Tusker were ready: twin tanks on their backs, a smaller bottle clipped under each arm, coils of hose for their two regulators across their chests like bandoliers. Tusker had strapped on a waterproof writing slate next to his dive computer on his right wrist. Sam wore a two-millimeter neoprene hood and checked the seal of her mask one last time before giving Tusker an OK sign. He wished he'd opted for a thicker suit. His two-millimeter suit was threadbare and used up. It would be little thermal protection against the chill at 350 feet and the hours of motionless hanging on the way back up.

He cursed his poor planning, then shook it out of his head and signaled back to Sam. They heaved themselves and the two hundred extra pounds of weight they carried onto the edge of the gunwale and tipped back clumsily into the sea.

"See you when I see you," Roland grinned over the side as they bobbed up, mercifully unweighted. Tusker had already put his regulator in his mouth and simply gave Roland a small nod before deflating his buoyancy wing and disappearing under the surface.

Dark Descent

Bay of Bengal, eight nautical miles east of Batticaloa, Sri Lanka.
The same day.

The descent took a full four minutes. They went down hand over hand, first pulling on the anchor line to break their initial buoyancy and then letting go, dropping as if pulled down by the invisible wreck below. Tusker took mental note of a light north-south current drawing him away from the taut yellow line. Decompression in a current could be difficult. He and Sam made occasional eye contact as they dropped, watching for telltale signs of mental or physical impairment and keeping an eye on tank valves and regulators for bubbles. Even a tiny leak at depth was cause for concern. They'd need every cubic foot of gas for their long decompression, or else they'd get bent or drown.

Tusker watched the numbers on his depth gauge tick off. The streams of sunlight, so friendly in the first 100 feet, gradually diminished to a flat grey at 150 feet, then to a sort of twilight below 200. As they approached 300, they switched on their hand-held torches against the blackness. Tusker aimed his below. The dark water absorbed most of the 5,000 lumens. No matter how many times Tusker had done these deep dives, he never got used to the apprehension of dropping into a black void. Besides the increasing pressure on his eardrums, which he occasionally relieved by wiggling his jaw from side to side, there was no sense of going up or down since there was no reference point in the dark water.

He felt the wreck before he saw it. It was an imperceptible change in the water column — the presence of something huge nearby. Then, his beam fell on a section of hull. The unmistakable shape of a ship, so out of place in this lonely spot. The *Vampire*. He reached up to his inflation hose and added a burst of gas into his buoyancy wing.

At this depth, and with four heavy tanks, the wing was almost fully inflated before it arrested his descent. He came to a stop just a foot above the coral-encrusted steel. Tusker made sure to stay as shallow as possible, near the top of the wreck. Even a few feet made a big difference in the minutes of deco time they'd have to spend on the way back up.

Sam drifted down next to him. Tusker searched her face to make sure she was doing OK. She wrinkled her eyes in a smile behind her mask and winked at him. He could see her taking in the wreck. The ship was huge, stretching well beyond their torch beams, which revealed only a few yards on either side of them.

The gas mixture they breathed contained less oxygen than air, the rest made up mostly of helium, an inert gas that doesn't have the narcotic effect that the nitrogen in air does. But helium is also a "cold" gas, meaning that the body loses heat faster through respiration than with air.

Tusker again cursed his decision not to wear a thicker suit. The temperature reading on his dive computer said 67 degrees, a full 20 degrees colder than at the surface. Tusker was used to cold water from his wreck diving in the Great Lakes, but there he wore insulation layers and a drysuit. For the ten-minute bottom time on the *Vampire,* he'd be fine, but he'd suffer on the long deco hang. *So be it.*

The anchor had hooked on the bow railing. Tusker had forgotten to account for this possibility. It meant a 100-yard swim to the aft end of the ship where the hole in the hull was, and then back again so they could ascend on the anchor line. This round trip would take up almost their entire planned bottom time. He gestured to Sam along the hull in the direction they needed to swim and set off in a measured flutter kick. Overexertion meant becoming hypoxic or using up their gas. In the thin beams of their twin torches, the swim felt interminable and disorienting, like walking in a railway tunnel lit only by a flashlight. Tusker paused every few kicks to make sure Sam was at his side. They were like two astronauts, spacewalking untethered away from their craft.

After five minutes, the hull below their torch beams curved down and away slightly as they approached the stern end of the shipwreck. The hole would come into view any moment now. *There!* Tusker shouted through his regulator and gestured. Sam nodded. He exhaled slightly, causing a decrease in his buoyancy, and descended towards the wound in the ship. He reached up and pressed the button to turn on the small GoPro camera he had secured to his harness, and confirmed that the red light was blinking.

Tusker ran his hand along the edge of the opening. It was blackened and jagged. There was no sign of an explosion or collision, just a neatly traced rectangle, clearly made by a cutting torch. He turned to make eye contact with Sam and held out his palm to tell her to stay put. She nodded. Tusker contorted his body upright and descended into the hole, fins first. The opening was big enough, but with the two smaller cylinders slung at his sides, it was an awkward move.

Then, a sharp pain that took a moment to register, his mind slushed from the cold and mild hypoxia. He glanced down and saw his wetsuit had torn away, exposing his shoulder. The black neoprene flapped and mingled with a black liquid. It was his own blood, snaking out of a cut on his white flesh. He'd scraped it along the razor sharp edge of the opening. Tusker gritted his teeth around the mouthpiece. Next time it might be his regulator hose or his buoyancy wing that tore. He felt a tap on top of his head and looked up. Sam was silhouetted above him in the hole. She flashed an urgent "OK" sign to him inquisitively. He returned the gesture and nodded, mustering a smile in the blinding beam of her torch.

The *Vampire* had come to rest on the sea floor at a steeply pitched angle. The inside of the hull where Tusker found himself was disorienting, made all the worse by the inky darkness. He cast his torch beam around the cavernous space. The ship's bottom was almost above him and anything that had been on the floor of this compartment was now piled in a chaotic jumble below him. Only his exhaled bubbles would guide him back up and to the way he came in. He was glad to have Sam just outside with her torch as some reference. He glanced at the timing ring of his Aquastar watch. Nine minutes, bottom time already! Every extra minute meant 15 minutes of decompression. He had to hurry. But what was he looking for? The helmet, yes, the helmet.

He swept the space with his torch. His own fin kicks had stirred up a cloud of silt, backscatter in the beam of light. But there, 15 feet below him, a flash of yellow. Yes! A Kirby Morgan Model 37, the most commonly used commercial diving helmet. Should he bring it up? What good would that do? It would be heavy and awkward to swim with and carry. *How had its owner managed to get out without it?* he wondered. From the back of the helmet trailed what looked like a twisted umbilical, like the kind that feeds electricity, comms, and breathing gas to a diver. The end of it lay coiled below, out of sight in the rubble. Near the helmet, another familiar object: a full dive suit! It had no sediment on it and, from Tusker's distance, looked almost new. The neck seal was split and the top of the suit torn as if ripped violently open by a superhuman force.

He had to go, but first made sure the red light on the GoPro was still flashing. He hoped the little camera had captured the scene despite the low light and sediment. Just as he started to ascend through this macabre chamber, a distinctive shape caught his eye. It looked like a small, fat rocket, with four fins on the tail and a bloated, bullet-shaped head. A series of what looked like valves or ports clustered around the midsection, with twisted piping connected to them.

It was a bomb alright, but not like any he'd seen before
in the holds of B-29s sunk in the Pacific. This one was
much bigger and fatter. It looked less aerodynamic. It was
bolted to what was left of a badly decomposed wooden
skid. Was the *Vampire* transporting munitions to the
Pacific theater? Trincomalee was a major Royal Navy base
during the war, so this wouldn't be unusual. But only
one, and way back here in the stern? Two limp yellow lift
bags hung off of a pair of rings on the bomb. These were
clearly modern. He could made out the JW Automarine
logo on one of them. It was all starting to make sense in
Tusker's muddled brain.

A loud clanging shook him from his thoughts. *Sam.*
It was time to go. He gave a last look at the bomb and
drifted upwards towards the opening, where he could see
the light of Sam's torch flicking to and fro, searching for
him. He aimed for her and found the inner lip of the hole
in the hull, reminding himself to be careful on the way
out. Something brushed his arm. Had Sam come inside to
find him?

He angled his torch towards whatever it was. A man was
looking back at him, screaming, six inches away. Tusker
gasped and violently pushed away, back down into the
hold. He was breathing hard. Sam was still clanging on
the outside. He aimed his torch again and sure enough,
there he was. A man, white and half naked, was pinned
against the inside top of the ship. His eyes were open and
bulging, his mouth a round "O". It was, Tusker reflected
grimly, the look of abject terror, the moment of death.

He shot up past the corpse and out of the opening. Sam was shouting incomprehensibly through her regulator, pointing at her dive computer. When she saw his face, she stopped. Unable to explain, he simply gestured back down the hull towards the bow and the anchor line. Tusker's dive computer read three hours, 28 minutes of decompression. The pressure gauge said his twin tanks were half empty. He didn't have time to calculate his air consumption rate, but knew it'd be close as to whether he'd have enough gas to last the full decompression time. He hoped Sam breathed less than him. Women typically did. Now it was a race against time, and one limited by every single inhalation.

The swim back felt easier, taking just half the time as the journey out. Tusker registered that the current must have strengthened. It acted like a tailwind, pushing them back to the bow. This helped for the swim but would make the ascent tricky. They'd have to hold fast to the anchor line so as not to be blown off the wreck and far away from the skiff above. If that happened, it would be up to Roland to recognize it and follow their bubbles on the surface in the boat.

Tusker saw the familiar stanchions of the forward-end railing and counted them off in his torch beam. The yellow anchor line would appear right about now. Yet he saw nothing.

Sam aimed her beam around, frantically searching for it. Had it come unhooked? Perhaps Roland had to reposition the skiff and re-hook the anchor on the wreck. Then, the light from Tusker's torch caught a flash of yellow in the water column. It was the anchor line, and he sighed with relief. But when he reached for it, he realized it had no tension. It was drifting in the current. He pulled and pulled and the line coiled in his hands until finally, the loose end of it appeared, splayed out in a fray of fibers. The anchor line had been cut.

Free Ascent

Somewhere off the east coast of Sri Lanka.
The same day.

A free ascent in open ocean is risky even without facing four hours of decompression time. Tusker knew this, but he also knew that they had no choice. Without an anchor line to orient themselves at the specific depths for a safe deco stop, they could drift, not only far off the wreck site, but also dangerously up or down in the water column, compromising their bodies' precious off-gassing. They would have to watch their depth gauges carefully, and each other.

He gave the thumbs-up sign to Sam and they began their ascent. He was already shivering from the cold. *God knows where we'll come to the surface*, he thought. All he knew was that with this north-south current, they'd come up well past Batticaloa and miles offshore. But before that, they had hours of desperate hanging in the water column, being pulled south like a wisp of seaweed.

Despite the impulse to hurry, Sam and Tusker slowly, deliberately ascended, no faster than 30 feet per minute, until they reached their first stop, prescribed by Tusker's Sherwood computer. The deco plan he'd scrawled on his wrist slate before the dive was obsolete given their added bottom time swimming the length of the wreck and searching for the anchor line. Now their safety was left to the dive computer's algorithms, which would adjust on the fly as they ascended. And that would only get them to the surface.

They hung at 120 feet for eight minutes. At least there was some light filtering down from the surface now. Tusker looked across at Sam. He could see the worry crease her face, even behind the mask and hood. She wasn't even supposed to be here. He wanted to reassure her that it would be OK, he'd somehow get them out of this, even though he knew it was a lie. He reached out and gripped both of her shoulders and gave them a squeeze. Her expression didn't change.

He thought of Sebastian, back at the Deep Blue. It was 3:30. He'd be back from diving the *Hermes* with the Russians and wonder where they were. Tusker wished he'd told someone else where they were going. At least then a search party could be mounted when they didn't return. It was basic safety on any expedition to tell a few people where you were going, but Tusker had been impulsive, reckless.

And what of Roland? Would he have dared to go back to the Deep Blue, or was he gone for good? Tusker was convinced now that he was somehow connected to all of this—the *Depth Charge*, the *Vampire*. Who knows, maybe he was even the one who'd blown up the *Taprobane*. Tusker vowed to find him. What he'd do when he did, he wasn't sure. But first, they had to somehow get ashore.

And at the moment, that possibility seemed remote.

The Sherwood beeped. Time to go up to the next stop.
80 feet for seven minutes. Tusker checked his pressure
gauge. He'd breathe down the big tanks as long as he
could, but soon they'd need something with a little
more oxygen to speed decompression. He glanced over
at Sam's gauges, upside down. She was fine. He found
himself studying her as they hung in the current. She
floated horizontal and motionless, her fins out behind her,
perfect form. Decompression was best if your entire body
was in the same plane, to allow equal off-gassing from all
tissues. Even here, behind the tangle of hoses and tanks,
she looked athletic and confident.

Beep. Time to ascend. At 60 feet, Tusker and Sam switched
to their 80-cubic-foot bottles of nitrox, a blend of 50%
oxygen and 50% nitrogen. The nitrogen would be nearly
harmless at this depth, and the extra oxygen would
accelerate their decompression. These tanks would have
to take them up to the 10 foot stop, where they'd finally
switch to a small tank of 100 percent oxygen. Tusker tried
to breathe evenly. He had to make this tank last close to
three hours.

And so they went on, being pulled south at progressively
shallower depths. Tusker was shivering noticeably now,
and Sam rubbed his arms. They were up to 30 feet and
the water was warm now, but the chill had gotten into
his core. He was also dehydrated from sucking dry gas
for three hours. His tank was down to 700 pounds per
square inch, less than a quarter of its contents remaining.
It would be a close call. He hoped he didn't need to ask

Sam for any of her gas.

At one point, the baritone gurgle of a boat motor seemed to come close and they both swiveled their heads, looking for it. It sounded too big to be Roland in the skiff and Tusker's hope faded when he realized there was nothing he could do anyway to signal it. Their only hope would be if someone saw their bubbles. But at dusk, in rolling ocean swells, this was unlikely. He wished he'd brought his reel. He could have hooked on his surface marker buoy to a line and sent it up with a puff of air to drift along with them, as some signal of their presence. Rookie mistake, not bringing it. He'd been in such a hurry to clandestinely load the skiff earlier that he'd forgotten it.

After three and a half hours, the Sherwood beeped again. It was nearly as dark now as it had been down on the wreck. They ascended to 10 feet, where they both switched regulators to finally breathe off of the small bottle of pure oxygen under their right arms. Tusker wiggled his limbs, trying to detect any telltale aches or pains that might be an early sign of decompression sickness. Aside from the throb in his shoulder where he'd been cut, and a stiff neck, he felt OK. They'd been careful. He was still cold and his lips felt cracked and dry. Neither of them had drunk any water for hours and who knew when they would have a chance to again. He wondered what they would see when they came to the surface. Would the shoreline be visible? Lights from a town along the coast or a boat?

At last, the Sherwood beeped a different tone. Tusker

shined his torch on its display: "All Clear." *God, I hope so*. He held his mask close to Sam's and nodded. She returned the nod and they kicked the remaining ten feet to the surface.

Adrift

Somewhere off the east coast of Sri Lanka.
That night.

There is no place more lonely and despairing than the
open ocean. Tusker and Sam surfaced into a moonless
night. The sea was black, the sky was black, the horizon
was black. They might as well have been in outer space.
Their chances of rescue were about as good out here.

"We need to shed these tanks and weights," Tusker
said. His voice was hoarse and it seemed strange to be
speaking after so many hours of anxious, nonverbal
communication underwater. His jaw hurt from biting
down on the rubber mouthpiece for so long. Both of them
were barely staying afloat, weighed down by their four
tanks plus weight belts. He was already unclipping his
two smaller cylinders from his harness. Sam did the same.

The more difficult task would be to remove the double
tanks on their backs while keeping their buoyancy wings
for flotation. The tanks were held together by aluminum
bands, then secured to their harnesses with long threaded
rods and wing nuts. It was finicky work even on the floor
of a well-lit workshop, but bobbing on the ocean, at night,
with frozen fingers, would be tricky. But the heavy tanks,

empty of their helium mix, were simply dead weight. It
had to be done.

Tusker switched on his dive torch and tucked it under
the shoulder strap of his harness, aiming it at the back
of Sam's tanks. The light was little use. The hardware
was under the water surface. He'd have to do it by feel.
First he twisted shut the tank valves and disconnected
the regulators, letting them hang loose. Then he reached
down between the tanks and found the end of the
threaded rod. The wing nut was on the inside of the
harness, under a pad at Sam's back.

"You're going to have to remove your harness for a bit,"
he said. "It'll be easier to disassemble it if it's floating in
front of me." Sam wriggled out of the shoulder straps
and the harness flopped over like a turtle and floated. "Be
sure to stay close to me," Tusker told her. "In the dark
especially, we don't want to get separated." Her thicker
wetsuit's buoyancy allowed her to float easily, and she
held on lightly to Tusker's own tanks while he worked.

After a few minutes, he had the wing nuts off and the
tanks fell immediately away, disappearing quickly into
the depths. The buoyancy wing popped up out of the
water like a pool toy, unencumbered by the unwieldy
cylinders. Sam slipped back into it, then helped Tusker
remove his gear. His thinner suit didn't offer as much
buoyancy on its own, and he struggled to keep his face
and arms above the surface while he fiddled with his
tanks. Finally, his tanks dropped into the abyss and he
cinched on his own harness and wing, panting from the
exertion of the awkward work.

"Small triumphs," he said to Sam.

"Thathi won't be happy we lost his tanks," she joked. "I think you've lost your security deposit."

"It's no use tiring ourselves out trying to swim right now," Tusker said. "We've got about eleven hours until any daylight, and I've no idea where we are in relation to shore."

Sam switched on her torch and aimed it at her arm. She had an old, square wrist compass lashed over her wetsuit sleeve with a long yellow nylon strap.

"Well, due west is…" she pivoted in the water, "that way." She held her arm out, which Tusker could barely make out. "So assuming the current was roughly to the south while we were decompressing, the coast should be over there."

"The question is, how far," Tusker said glumly. "The *Vampire* was already about eight miles offshore."

"Our best hope is the fishing fleet, come morning," she replied. "Let's save our torch batteries and if we hear a boat, we can raise our marker buoys and shine our lights on them. Hope someone's paying attention."

Tusker was lying on his back, as if on a raft. The buoyancy wing was more than enough to keep him afloat, but the wing pushed him face-down unless he kicked. Every once in a while, the clouds parted and he caught sight of a few stars.

"Anything dangerous out here, Miss Marine Biologist?" he called out in the darkness. He thought of the hundreds of fathoms of black water under his dangling feet.

"Not really," she replied. "We get the occasional Portuguese man o' war, but the shark fin trade has been merciless on anything big with teeth out here. Well, unless you count the sperm whales."

"So, what do you think happened to Roland?" Sam asked. "That anchor line looked like it was cut."

"Could have been any number of things," Tusker replied. "If the current got strong at the surface, or the swells got big, it could have been tough for him to keep the boat in place. The anchor line could have chafed and finally parted on the gunwale…"

"Or he could have cut it intentionally," she said coldly.

"What makes you think that?" Tusker asked, surprised at her tone. "Is there something about Roland I don't know?"

"He showed up a few months back and offered to help Thathi in exchange for free room and board and some occasional diving," Sam said. "But I think he's into something else."

"Like what?"

"I don't know. He comes and goes at odd times with some shifty-looking guys. And then there were the girls." She paused. "I saw him in Batticaloa once handing a wad of

147

cash to one that looked suspiciously young. I've also seen him chatting up schoolgirls."

"Yeah, I gathered he's a bit of a pig," Tusker said, remembering how he was leering at Anja, the Swedish girl. "But cutting the anchor line is a bit more serious than being a dirty old man."

"He also seemed a little too interested in what Upali was doing here. Asked a lot of questions about their plans, what they were looking for."

"Your father seemed to tolerate him." Tusker tried to give him the benefit of the doubt. Maybe help was on the way. Leaving them adrift on the ocean was tantamount to attempted murder.

"Thathi needed the help and was willing to look the other way," she said. "I used to be around a lot more to help with the resort and the divers. But with my work and all the traveling…"

They floated in silence for a while. At the surface the water was warm and, even with the breeze and his exhaustion, it wasn't entirely unpleasant. The swells had become gentle and lapped at the top of his head, where it was tipped back in the water. It reminded Tusker of summer nights swimming in the shallow lake at his family's cabin in Michigan. But here, of course, the next landfall south of Sri Lanka is Antarctica.

Tusker opened his eyes. Had he fallen asleep? *Damn it!*
He bolted upright with a splash and swiveled around in
the darkness. "Sam!" he called. No answer. "Sam!"
Again, louder. In the distance, he saw a flicker. A pin
prick of light danced at water level. Sam. He flipped
onto his back and kicked hard, doing an awkward but
effective backstroke in the direction of the light. Every
now and then he stopped and sat up to make sure he was
going the right way. The light was getting bigger
now, and he could hear Sam calling his name and
splashing towards him.

After 15 minutes of hard swimming, they came
together in a clumsy, panting embrace. "Oh god, Sam,
I'm so sorry."

"Me too, me too," she replied. He buried his face in her
wet hair and clutched her hard to him.

"We've got to stay together. We can sleep in shifts," he
said with newfound authority. He peered at the hands of
his watch. 1:30. Four more hours until dawn. It would be
light earlier than that.

The adrenaline from the swim had woken him up. He
didn't let go of Sam's waist. He knew her face was
directly in front of his, though he could only make out the
silhouette of her head. On an impulse, he leaned in and
kissed her hard, where he thought her mouth was.

"Owww!" she shouted as they knocked foreheads. They
both burst out laughing. He let go of her waist and
backed away but clutched her hand. They lay back on the

water, still breathing hard. The clouds had cleared and the sky was a black canvas, pinned with bright stars.

"Do you know your constellations?" Tusker finally asked. "I know the usual suspects, but this close to the equator, it gets a little more confusing. Or maybe we've even drifted into the Southern Hemisphere by now."

"I know a few," she replied. "My mother used to teach me..." Her voice trailed off.

"She was killed," she said, before he could ask. Her voice was cold suddenly. "She was working at the World Trade Center in Colombo when a Tamil Tiger suicide bomber walked in and blew himself up."

"Wow, I'm so... sorry." Tusker's reply felt feeble.

Sam continued. "She was a wonderful woman. I was only 11 when she died, but I remember how kind she was. Always told me I could do anything with my life. Thathi says I remind him of her."

"I'm sure she'd be very proud of who you've become," Tusker said. "Your father never remarried?"

"He never was the same after she died. She was the love of his life."

Tusker gave her hand a squeeze. "Why don't you sleep a bit," he said. "I'm wide awake now and can keep an eye out."

"We're going to be OK, right?" Her voice sounded small, vulnerable.

"Of course," he lied. "Come morning, I'm sure we'll see we're only a few hundred meters off of a perfect white sand beach."

She didn't laugh, or reply. But even in the dark, Tusker could tell she wasn't asleep.

Strange Catch

Pottuvil, Sri Lanka.
The next morning.

It was another bad haul, and now the motor was acting
up. Chandin had been coaxing it along for months,
cleaning the spark plugs and adding oil every night.
It was only a matter of time before it would need an
overhaul. But with the fishing so bad, it was all he could
do to pay for his gas from the day's catch. Every night,
he sailed his 32-foot trawler further out, hoping to find
a new reef or fishing ground that no one had discovered
yet. One shark would feed his family for a month and pay
for the motor's repair, but he hadn't caught one in years.

The anemic engine chugged along at half its usual rpms.
It would be well past 8:00 when they'd get back to the
beach and another hour before he'd have his small pile
of kingfish, barracuda, and squid at the market. Ajith, his
son, slept curled up in the bow on a heap of old nets, still
with the peace of youth, unencumbered by the worry that
plagued Chandin.

The boat wallowed over the lazy swells, and the sun
rose over Chandin's left shoulder. Seven miles ahead,
the shoreline appeared in the morning haze of sea spray,

wood smoke and diesel exhaust. Another fishing boat was on the horizon to the south, angling in towards Pottuvil. He recognized the gaily painted cabin as that of Mulan and wondered what kind of night he'd had. *Looks like he went out far too*, thought Chandin.

He heard a faint shout, barely audible above the chugging engine. He cut the rpms and listened. There it was again. It couldn't have been Mulan. He was too far away, but he didn't see another boat. He reduced to idle speed and came out on the front deck, stepping deftly over the fishing tackle with his bare feet. "Ajith!" He gave him a nudge and the boy sat up and rubbed his eyes. "I heard something. Help me look." He spoke in Tamil.

The sea was still grey in the morning light, with a few whitecaps rolling towards the distant coast. Fifty meters off the starboard bow he caught a flash of color. It disappeared below a roller, then reappeared. It was a bright orange tube, somehow floating vertically in the water. Then — yes! — a person. Two people, in fact, both waving their arms at him. What were they doing this far offshore, and this early in the morning? Had their boat capsized? He shouted back to them and ran to the cabin, shouting to Ajith to keep an eye on them.

Chandin pushed the throttle forward and the motor sluggishly came to life. He spun the wheel to swing the boat near to them, then cut the motor to idle speed and drifted up alongside.

The white man said something in a choked, hoarse voice. It was English, and Chandin couldn't understand. He could see that the man's lips were cracked and his face was weathered and pale. The woman looked drugged, barely able to hold on to the side of the boat. How long had they been in the water? Ajith and Chandin leaned over the side and awkwardly pulled them on board. The big man tumbled on to the deck and lay there, contorted and shivering. The father and son were able to hoist the woman fairly easily and they leaned her against the netting in the bow. Both of them wore wetsuits and diving fins, which Chandin quickly wrenched off their feet.

"Ajith, water!" he instructed tersely in Tamil. Ajith ran to the cabin and came back with a full two-liter plastic bottle. Chandin took it from him and poured some into the woman's mouth. She gulped at it and then gagged and vomited on the deck. "*Himming, himming,*" Chandin said in Sinhala, hoping she would understand. She nodded weakly and drank again, this time swallowing. Chandin did the same for the man, who had managed to pull himself next to the woman and prop himself up. He held the water in his mouth for a while before swallowing.

Chandin ran back to the cabin and pushed the throttle forward, bringing the old boat to life. He decided to risk the motor. These people were in rough shape. The bow wallowed at first, then careened up and over each successive swell. The shoreline drew closer and he could see men out raking the sand in front of the tourist hotels. As he neared the small beach just south of the point, he throttled back and, without pausing, motored through the cut in the reef. Normally he wouldn't take it so fast, but he'd done this a thousand times and knew exactly where his hull would make it without scraping bottom.

"Ajith, quickly, throw out the anchor!" His son was already waiting with the small grapple in his hand and he threw it over the side, then took up the slack to hold the boat fast in four feet of water. Chandin cut the motor and came out of the cabin. He and Ajith roused the man and woman. Their Tamil was met with blank stares. "Ajith, take an arm," Chandin said, and threaded his own arm under the woman's. A small crowd of fishermen had gathered in the waist-deep water at the beach. Chandin beckoned them to help and two rail-thin men waded out to the boat. Chandin and Ajith lowered the woman over the side into the water into the men's arms. They carried her to the beach and set her alongside a small skiff that had been pulled up there, then ran back out for the man.

"This one's heavy," Chandin said, and he and Ajith half lowered, half dropped the man into the water, where the two fishermen struggled to keep him upright, dragging him by his armpits up next to the woman. Ajith followed, carrying the diving fins.

"Who are they?"
"Where did they come from?"
"What will you do with them?" The crowd had grown around the couple slumped on the sand, passed out.

Chandin raised his hands to the group and calmly said, "They are in a bad way. If a few of you will kindly help, we will take them to our house, give them something to eat and drink, and let them sleep. Then we will see how to get them home."

155

The Kindness of Strangers

Pottuvil, Sri Lanka.
That evening.

Tusker awoke to the smell of food. It was both incredibly
appetizing and revolting. Pungent fish, oil, spices.
Nearby, he could hear the clanging of a spoon in a pan,
something frying.

Where was he? His eyes adjusted to the dark, and he
lifted his head to look around. He was lying on a low
bed in a small room. It was almost completely
unadorned, with whitewashed walls and a single
high window with flimsy curtains. Across from him,
against the wall, was a table with a small statue on it.
He recognized it as the Hindu god, Ganesha, with its
distinctive elephant's head. Sticks of incense stood unlit
around it and a garland of flowers was draped over the
back of the makeshift shrine.

Next to him, he heard a groan. Sam was lying on an
identical bed across from his. She stirred and rolled
over. "Where are we?" she whispered. Tusker sat up and
reached across to her. He stroked her hair.

"I don't know, but we're alive," he said. "I've got a

pounding headache. Must be dehydration." A bottle of water sat on the floor between the beds and he reached for it.

"We don't know how clean that is," Sam said to him. "I'm used to drinking the water here, but if you get diarrhea, it'll only dehydrate you more."

"I'm willing to risk that," he chuckled. "I swallowed so much seawater, I'm desiccated." He chugged at the bottle. It tasted of iodine. Someone had thoughtfully purified it for them. He passed it to Sam and she drank deeply from it.

"Slide over," Tusker said and shimmied on to Sam's bed. It was barely big enough for one, and groaned under his added 200-pound weight.

"Don't you think we should go find out where we are?" Sam whispered, leaning up on one elbow to look at him. Tusker was shirtless, still in his swim trunks. She wore her bikini, but with a loose salwar top on over it. She didn't know how she'd gotten it. Even in the dark, she could see the creases in Tusker's face, his cracked lips. She licked her own and then bent over and kissed him. He put his arm around her and pulled her down. She laid with her head on his shoulder and draped her arm over his naked stomach. His skin was cool and she could feel the dried salt on it. The smell of his sweat excited her.

"You need a bath," she said in a scolding whisper and feigned pushing him away. He pulled her tighter and she giggled. Tusker could feel her breasts against his side and her soft hair on his shoulder. He closed his eyes. They laid like that, clutching each other, for a long time.

When he awoke, Sam was still draped across him, breathing deeply. He held up his arm and squinted at his watch. 6:20. Day or night? He had lost all sense of time. He could only vaguely recall being hauled out of the sea in the morning, but he couldn't be sure which day. He gently lifted Sam's arm, laid it down on the hard mattress, and stood up. His legs ached, cramped from being in the water for so long. From the next room, he could hear a TV or radio playing. Hindi music. He was suddenly ravenous. *When was the last time we ate?* He slipped across the cool concrete floor to the doorway, which was hung with a simple rod and fabric curtain. He peered out. A small woman was standing at a two-burner gas cooker, stirring something. His sudden appearance startled her.

"Hello!" Tusker said and smiled, hoping to put her at ease. She nodded and bowed slightly, avoiding eye contact. She could have only come up to his chest and weighed maybe 85 pounds. In this tiny house, where his head nearly reached the ceiling, Tusker must have seemed a giant.

She spoke. "Tea?" She held up a chipped cup.

"Yes, please," Tusker replied and nodded exaggeratedly. She didn't seem to speak English, but lifted the pot from the burner and poured it expertly into the cup. It was pale with powdered milk already added, and when she handed him the cup, it was scalding hot. "*Isthuthi,*" he said, hoping she spoke Sinhala, though he suspected this was a Tamil household, judging from the Hindu shrine in the bedroom. She looked at him and smiled.

She said something to him in Tamil. He shook his head quizzically. *"Badagini?"* she repeated, this time in Sinhala. Hungry? He nodded again, and she smiled and gestured for him to sit at the small table in the room. It was a tiny house. The dining table sat opposite the tiny cooking space and beyond it, a sitting room with a simple rattan bench, some pillows, and a few plastic chairs. In the corner of the room was a rolled-out mat and some sheets. This is where she had slept, presumably with the fisherman who'd rescued them. They'd given up their own room for him and Sam.

The woman scraped at some pots in the kitchen and turned to hand Tusker a plate heaped with rice and some curries. He sat at the table and without a word tucked into the steaming food with his fingers. The food, a few vegetables cooked in coconut milk, lentils, and dried fish, was spicy and delicious. Tusker wiped the sweat from his brow with his forearm between bites. The woman stood and watched him from the kitchen. When he finished, he sat back in the chair and exhaled. She set a small bowl of lime water in front of him to wash his fingers. *"Hari hondai,"* he grinned, his face flushed. He felt human again. The woman smiled back at him.

"Oyage nona?" she gestured to the room. She thought Sam was his wife. Tusker nodded and stood up. He exaggeratedly tiptoed to the room and held back the curtain. In the light from the other room, he could see that

Sam was awake. She was sitting up, rubbing her eyes.

"I just had the best meal of my life," he said to her. "I don't know who these people are, but they gave us their room and she just fed me enough food for an entire family."

"That's the way it usually is here," Sam replied. "The ones with the least to give, give the most."

She stood up and brushed past Tusker, letting her hand linger on his chest as she passed him in the doorway. It was now 7:30, a full day since they'd been brought ashore. They'd slept an entire day and the following night. Where they'd ended up, he didn't know, but it was a stroke of luck that the fisherman happened upon them.

"Pottuvil," Sam called out to him, as if knowing what he was wondering. She'd been talking to the woman while sitting with her own plate of food. "My Tamil's not great, but she says her husband and son brought us in yesterday. Her name is Devika and her husband is Chandin. Their son is Ajith." The woman smiled and nodded at Tusker as she heard the names. "They're still out fishing now."

"Wow, we drifted a long way!" Tusker exclaimed. "Your father must be worried sick."

"Yeah, I should call the Deep Blue and at least tell him we're alive. They don't have a phone, but apparently we're not too far from a guest house and we can walk over and make a call there. I can ask Thathi to send someone to pick us up."

"Good point," Tusker said. "I hate to impose on these people any further. Any chance there's a place we can have a bath before we set off?"

"She said they've got a small outdoor tap we can use and some soap," Sam said. "It's not much, but like I said, you could sure use it." She winked at Tusker. He grinned back at her. Devika walked to a small dresser and opened the top drawer. She pulled out two cotton sarongs and handed one to Sam and one to Tusker.

"Make sure you tie it correctly," Sam said to Tusker. "She'll kick us out if you have a wardrobe malfunction."

Tusker laughed as he walked to the side door. "No guarantees!"

The tap was at waist height, on a naked pipe coming out of the side of the house and perched above a slab of cracked concrete. It was dark besides the light from the window and Tusker cautiously looked around before slipping out of his swim trunks. The water was cold but felt good on his salt-dried skin. He lathered up with the tiny sliver of soap and then rinsed off and shut off the tap. He was dripping wet but with no towel to dry off, he reached for the sarong, which hung on a peg nearby. When he turned, Sam was there. In the shadows, he could see that she was also naked.

"My turn," she said quietly with a smile. She walked past him to the tap, trailing her hand along his naked flank. "Go inside and wait for me," she said firmly. "And be careful," she said, eyeing him below the waist. That sarong doesn't leave much to the imagination. We don't want to scare our poor hostess."

A Father's Secret

Aberdeen, Scotland.
Two years earlier.

Malcolm Rausing rarely stepped foot on dry land. He preferred the freedom of the open sea, with its murky and arcane laws. Rausing Oceanic's ships were built by the lowest bidder, paid for by the highest bidder, flagged in Panama or Liberia, operated by Pakistanis and Filipinos and largely immune from oversight or prosecution. The high seas were the last frontier, the Wild West, and that was just the way Rausing liked it.

When he decided it was time to shutter the company's *de facto* headquarters once and for all, Malcolm Rausing sailed into Aberdeen aboard his latest ship, the DSV *Depth Charge,* to pay a final visit. The office, in a harbor-front building that once looked out on the company's fleet, sat neglected, its view now blocked by shiny condominiums. It was staffed by an underpaid skeleton crew of secretaries and cleaning crew who rarely showed up to work. Rausing ordered all of the company's legacy documentation be digitized and then destroyed. This was all to be done secretly by employees promised a lucrative pension. Only his personal office, once Angus Rausing's, was to be left untouched. He would look to that.

His father's old desk was a massive oak affair, built from leftover timber from Rausing Oceanic's first ship in the 1950s. Its surface was scarred and covered with a film of dust and heaped with unopened mail. A scrimshaw letter opener lay in a tray beneath a green shaded lamp and an assortment of nautical paraphernalia lined the corners, booty salvaged by Angus during his time as a diver. Malcolm Rausing hated this place. It was drafty and dark and smelled of the past, a past he never knew, yet disdained. His father's portrait glowered from the reception area. *Burn it with the rest*, Rausing thought.

In a locked lower drawer of the desk was his father's dive logbook. Malcolm had never bothered to look at it. He'd heard enough of his father's war stories of diving in far flung places, refloating sunken ships, de-mining harbors, and retrieving bodies. But before tossing it on to the growing pile of papers to be destroyed, something compelled him to open it. He flipped its wrinkled, stained pages, mostly scratched with depths, bottom times, and locations, until he reached the final entry, scrawled in a shaky hand that he recognized as that of his crippled father:

Ceylon. 15 April, 1942. Vampire *salvage, 59 fathoms.*

It had been his last dive — killed his partner, too. Angus Rausing had told Malcolm little about it, and he'd only pieced together sketchy details. He read the last line in the dive log's final entry:

Weapon. Aft bomb room. Atomic?

He thumbed the pages thoughtfully. Ceylon. *What did they call it now? Yes, Sri Lanka.* He slipped the logbook into his briefcase, clicked off the lamp and strode out of the office. "I'm finished here," he said to no one in particular, shutting the door behind him.

A month after Rausing sailed out of Aberdeen for the last time, the offices of Rausing Oceanic burned to the ground. Local authorities traced the cause to some old wiring and insurance paid out £2 million. By the following spring, the footings for new condominiums had been laid on the property.

Chance Encounter

Four miles south of Batticaloa, Sri Lanka.
Present day.

The taxi rattled off, its loud exhaust coughing well into the distance. Tusker and Sam stood slightly dazed in front of the Deep Blue Resort, both in sarongs, their diving fins and buoyancy harnesses at their feet. It was two in the afternoon and the place was quiet.

The old cook was peeling potatoes and looked up as she entered, startled to see her. He clutched her in a tight, awkward embrace and then stepped towards Tusker, who stood behind her. He thought twice about hugging him, but nodded his head and smiled a toothless grin. Sam exchanged excited words with him in Sinhala.

"Thathi went up to Trincomalee after we called this morning to talk to the navy about what happened," she said to Tusker. "We should get changed and get up there. I'll drive." She left the kitchen and hurried to her room. Tusker jogged to catch up.

"Did the cook say where Roland is?"

"He's gone," she said tersely. "Never came back, apparently."

Tusker nodded. "I'll grab Upali's laptop so we can show the ROV footage to someone at the navy. That should spur some action."

The GoPro he'd taken on their *Vampire* dive was now somewhere at the bottom of the ocean, having fallen off during their long night of drifting. The ROV video of the helmet would have to suffice. Tusker set off in a jog towards his room.

Someone had been there. The room wasn't any messier than he'd left it, but his backpack was not hanging on the back of the door. Upali's computer bag was on Ian's bed. The laptop was gone. He'd have normally suspected a burglary, but Ian's Omega watch was still sitting on the bedside table next to his passport. Tusker quickly changed into a polo shirt and fresh khaki shorts and left to find Sam.

Ten minutes later, they were bashing down the road from the Deep Blue in the Land Rover. The truck lurched and bounced violently on the ruts and potholes. As they reached the junction with the main road, Tusker reached for a seatbelt.

"Sorry," she said while looking over her shoulder for an opening in the traffic, "this one's ex-military. They stripped out any amenities, including the seatbelts. You'll have to trust my driving." He saw himself reflected in her sunglasses as she smirked at him.

Sam swung the Land Rover through a roundabout, expertly double-clutching a downshift into second gear

166

and sneaking in ahead of a groaning Leyland bus. As they gained speed, a hot breeze blew in through the crude cabin vent flaps and sliding windows, doing little to counteract the sweat that poured freely down Tusker's face.

"What do you think your father can get the navy to do?" Tusker shouted above the din of the engine and road noise.

"Thathi used to serve in the navy," she replied. "He's got an old pal that works at the base. I'm not sure what they can do, but it'll be good to have their support."

Tusker's damp shirt was sticking to the vinyl seat back. It was too loud to carry on a conversation and they drove in silence. He glanced across at Sam. She had put on the same olive colored shorts he'd first seen her in and a ribbed tank top with no bra underneath. Her neck and chest shimmered with a mist of perspiration. She'd kicked off her rubber slippers when she got into the Land Rover, and her bare feet worked the clutch, brake, and gas pedals as she rowed through the gears. He found the whole scene somehow erotic and he reached across and put his hand on her bare thigh. It was cool and firm.

"Is this what you call, in America, distracted driving?" She flashed a smile without taking her eyes off the road.

Tusker closed his eyes and thought back to the night before, in the small bed, their hands quietly learning each other's bodies in the dark. *Baila* music played in the next room. He traced the outline of her firm breasts, felt the stubble under her arms and the moistness between her legs. She had silently rolled over and straddled him. The whole thing hadn't lasted long, and they lay side by side panting quietly, going to sleep without a word.

"We need to stop for gas." Sam's voice jolted Tusker upright. They were passing through Pasikudah, the last big town between Batticaloa and Trincomalee. The streets were choked with all manner of people and animals on the move—tuk-tuks, taxis, buses, bicycles, and cattle. It was slow going. Sam used the horn liberally as she ground the Land Rover into second, then third, the gearbox protesting with a crunch. Finally, she turned into a Ceypetco service station on a street corner and switched off the engine. An attendant ambled over to the open window and she handed him a sheaf of rupee notes.

"I'm roasting," Tusker said as he peeled himself off the seat. "I'm going to run over to that shop and grab some bottles of water." He jumped down from the truck and jogged across the road, dodging a swaying lorry that blasted a warning with its triple air horns.

The shop was sweltering and smelled of rotting fish. Several women floated up and down the small aisles in sarees and a bored-looking man sat behind the counter waving flies away. Tusker walked to a small refrigerated case at the back of the shop and took out four small plastic bottles of ice cold water. While he was waiting to pay, he looked out at the bright street. He could see Sam sitting in the Land Rover as the attendant finished filling the tank. A large vehicle flashed across his view. It was one of those oversized Toyota SUVs, a deluxe version with tinted glass and large tires. It came to a stop two doors down from the gas station at a branch office of the Royal Ceylon Bank. A man stepped out on to the road. A Western man in a red cap. It was Roland, and the cap he was wearing was Tusker's.

"Bastard..." muttered Tusker through clenched teeth.

"Sir?" The man at the checkout said to Tusker, who looked down and clumsily handed over some cash.

"Keep the change," Tusker said, taking the water bottles in his hand and moving towards the door, not taking his eyes off that Toyota. He glanced over at the gas station. Sam had started the Land Rover and was easing it onto the road, waiting to turn left and come across to pick him up. He hoped Roland wouldn't see her. He wanted to see what he was up to first.

Roland was talking to a man in the left hand passenger side window of the Toyota, someone Tusker couldn't see. He smiled and nodded. Then the door opened and a man stepped out onto the curb. He was tall and fair, with swept-back silver hair, a turtleneck and trousers. When he shielded his face against the harsh sun, an expensive watch glinted on his wrist. The man was a full head taller than Roland. It was Rausing.

As I suspected, Tusker thought to himself. Roland *was* connected to Rausing. He stood in the shade of the shop and continued to watch the two men, debating whether to confront Roland. Suddenly, a car horn blared. It was Sam in the Land Rover. She was double parked in the middle of the road, waving to Tusker to get in. He looked back at Roland and the man. The sound had made them look and Roland was staring right at Tusker with his mouth open. Rausing was frowning. Tusker quickly ran to the Land Rover and jumped into the passenger seat.

"Go," he said to Sam, sternly. "Now!" She engaged the clutch and the truck narrowly dodged a bicycle. As they sped past the Toyota, Rausing fixed his pale eyes on Tusker under steeply arched brows. The Land Rover careened around a roundabout and roared north out of Pasikudah.

Car Trouble

Pasikudah, Sri Lanka.
Later that day.

Sam kept the gas pedal of the Land Rover pressed to the floor. The underpowered truck hurtled up the A15 in a cacophony of rattles and whining gears. Tusker looked back, expecting to see the black Land Cruiser right behind them, but it didn't materialize.

"I think we're fine, you can let up," he shouted over to Sam. Normal conversation was difficult in this truck at idle; above 40 miles per hour, it was nearly impossible. She nodded and let off the accelerator.

Suddenly, there was a loud bang and the Land Rover skidded to the right, careening across the road and narrowly missing a tuk-tuk headed the other direction.

"What the hell!" Tusker yelled as he was pitched across the slippery vinyl seats. Sam jammed on the brakes and wrestled the steering wheel to bring the truck to a stop just before it tipped into a grassy ditch.

Sam shut off the ignition and leaned her forehead on the steering wheel, exasperated, but didn't say anything.

"What was it?" Tusker asked. "What was that bang? Did we hit something?"

Sam shook her head and looked out the windscreen at the traffic they were now facing. "Sounded like a blown diff."

"The differential?" Tusker said. Sam nodded and opened the door. Tusker followed. There was an acrid smell of burnt rubber and hot metal and a fresh streak of black leading from the middle of the highway to where the truck now sat. A lorry streaked by, its wind horn gaily calling in full Doppler effect.

"I'm just glad this happened when the traffic is light," Tusker gestured to the passing lorry. Sam didn't reply but dropped to her hands and knees and peered under the Land Rover.

"I'm guessing you don't have any sort of roadside assistance for this thing," he said.

Sam ignored his comment. "There's a mechanic back in Pasikudah who's good with these Landies. If we can limp into town, I bet he's got a spare differential lying about."

"I don't think it'll move, much less limp," Tusker said.

"Nah, it'll get us there," Sam smiled confidently and jumped up, brushing gravel from her knees. She went back to the passenger seat and lifted off the cushion revealing a storage box. She slid off the cover, pulled out a rolled-up canvas pouch, and dropped it on the ground. A crowd had gathered now, a few skinny kids and an old man on a bicycle.

"I'm going to need you to support the driveshaft while I disconnect it from the differential," Sam said and dropped to the ground again. She fished out a handful of open-end wrenches and slid under the truck so that only her bare legs extended out. Tusker went around to the other side and joined her underneath. The metal was hot and there was already a puddle of oil collecting under the gearbox.

Sam tried a couple of wrenches before finding the right fit and grunted as she twisted on the bolts that held the driveshaft into the rear differential housing. Tusker watched her work admiringly. She caught his look.

"Make yourself useful and hold up the driveshaft," she told him. "It's gonna come loose here shortly, and be careful. It's a lot heavier than you think it will be."

When the last bolt came out, the full weight of the shaft dropped onto Tusker's hands. She was right, it was heavy.

"OK, just hang on for a bit while I rig up some wire to support it." She slid out from under the truck and he could hear her fishing around in the tool roll. Tusker's arms started to quiver from the weight. He could see Sam's legs and those of all the spectators on the road side of the vehicle. The crowd had grown.

Sam dropped back down and joined Tusker underneath. She was clutching a wad of wire and a snips. "You doing OK there?" she smiled at Tusker, who was sweating profusely, both from the effort and his proximity to the hot exhaust pipe. "Fancy a tea break?"

"Just get on with it!" he barked back.

Sam laughed and wiped her nose, leaving a black streak of grease. She threaded the wire around the driveshaft and then up around the crossmember of the truck's chassis. After four loops, she told him to let go. The wire held. Sam cut the excess wire and shimmied out. Tusker followed. The old man rolled his bike forward and said something to Sam in Tamil, smiling toothlessly. Sam replied and the two shared a hearty laugh.

"What did he say?" Tusker scowled, feigning hurt at being left out of the joke.

"Oh, something to the effect of what a capable and confident man you are for helping me," she winked. "Now give me the keys. Let's get going."

Sam put the Land Rover in neutral and started the motor, then pushed a red lever forward to engage low-range four-wheel drive. Now, instead of the rear wheels driving the truck, the front wheels would pull them back to town. She eased them back onto the highway, where traffic had swelled in the hour it took to make the repair, and steered the Land Rover back towards town.

It was a slow journey. Sam nursed the Land Rover the few miles into town in fourth gear, barely topping 15 miles per hour. Tuk-tuks, cars, and even bicycles passed them. Tusker kept a wary eye out for Rausing's black Land

Cruiser as they entered Pasikudah but it was nowhere to be seen. The truck lurched through one roundabout after another until Sam finally coasted down a narrow side street lined with shop stalls, pedestrians, and parked vehicles.

"There it is," she said and pointed out a stall with a sign above it in Arabic and English. "*Majeed Motor Repairs Pvt.*," it read. A faded Union Jack was painted next to the name. An articulated metal overhead door was partially open and inside was another Land Rover, its wheels removed, perched atop jack stands. Stacks of tires lined the inside, along with various vehicle parts, including an intact engine on a wooden pallet. The bright flash of a welding torch emanated from the darkness at the back of the shop. "Another week and we'd be out of luck. Ramadan."

Sam parked in front of the garage, honked the horn and shut off the engine. A man emerged from within, squinting in the bright daylight. He was a slight man with a wiry grey beard. He wore the white skull cap of practicing Muslims, but instead of a traditional long tunic, he had on a mechanic's jumpsuit. It was filthy. When he caught sight of Sam, he broke into a smile.

"Ahmed!" Sam called out as she climbed from behind the wheel. Tusker got out and stretched. The man Tusker assumed was Ahmed Majeed approached Sam with his arms wide, then stopped short.

"I'm dirty," he said, "I don't want to get you covered in grease."

"Ah, come on, so am I," Sam said, and embraced him. The two of them chatted excitedly while Tusker stood awkwardly by. "Oh, sorry, this is Tusk, er, Julian Tusk, a friend who's staying with us at the Deep Blue for a while." Sam stepped back and Tusker extended his hand. Majeed grasped it with both of his and shook warmly.

"Nice to meet you, Mr. Majeed," Tusker said. "Everyone calls me Tusker."

"How do you do, Tusker? But I'm not Majeed." he replied. "My name is Ahmed Raheem."

"Ah, I just assumed from the sign," Tusker gestured up. Ahmed nodded.

"I sort of inherited the shop from Majeed." He hesitated. "The family moved to Dubai after Mrs. Majeed died during the troubles."

Tusker looked from Ahmed to Sam and back. There was an extended silence. Just before he could say anything, Ahmed gestured.

"I was about to put the kettle on," he said. "Let's have some tea and you can tell me what brought you." The broad smile was back.

An hour later, after a cup of tea and some sweet biscuits that Ahmed's wife had produced, they walked back out to the shop. It was approaching midday. Despite the heat, the street was packed with people going about their business.

"It should take me about two hours to swap the differential," Ahmed said. "And when was the last time you changed the fluids in this old thing?" he looked at Sam. She sheepishly looked down. "I'll throw that in too. Make it three hours. Meanwhile, take Mr. Tusker up the road to get some crab curry. You know that shop at the top of the road does a good one."

Sam and Tusker set off on foot, leaving Ahmed to fix the Land Rover. The two of them were quite the curious pair in this largely Muslim town and they drew stares as they walked.

"I didn't want to ask Ahmed, but what happened to the previous owners of his shop?" Tusker finally asked.

Sam stopped walking and looked at him. "After the Easter bombings a couple years ago, there was a backlash of violence against Muslims, especially here in the East. Shops torched, people beaten, mosques vandalized… the government did little to help."

She glanced back and then continued, "The Majeeds had been here for decades. My father used to take this same Land Rover to him for repairs back in the '90s. Then during the violence here, someone threw a petrol bomb into the shop and with all the flammable fluids stored in there, it burned pretty quickly. Majeed tried to get his wife out but…" Her voice trailed off. "Anyway, after that, he moved to Dubai to live with his daughter and her family. Ahmed worked for Majeed for years and took over the shop."

They continued on up the street to where it intersected with the main road. Pasikudah is an old town and shows battle scars from many years of strife. It was a stronghold of the Tamil Tigers during the civil war and was pounded by the country's military before peace finally arrived in 2009. By then, decades of neglect had left its infrastructure in tatters. The country's Muslim population found some solace here, far from the populous west coast, Colombo and the Buddhist Hill Country around Kandy. But then came the more recent violence. Some storefronts were blackened from fire or simply abandoned or boarded up. Still, the streets were lively, with men in long tunics and caps and women, most in hijab but some in full burqa.

Over steaming bowls of crab curry, Sam filled Tusker in on the complicated background of the Buddhist-Muslim tensions in Sri Lanka.

"So the government tolerates this militant Buddhist group?" Tusker asked, his lips on fire from the curry.

"Some say the government is even behind them, covertly, of course." Sam said, deftly cracking a claw open. She sucked the meat out and discarded the shell on a side plate.

"People wanted blood revenge against the Muslims after the Easter bombings, and the new government was elected on that veiled promise. The Buddhist Power Army has been terrorizing Muslims here for years on a small scale, but lately have gotten emboldened. The government is happy to look the other way. The Muslims here live in fear."

Tusker looked around. Pasikudah seemed like a peaceful enough town, and he still had a hard time imagining Buddhist monks throwing Molotov cocktails. The curry was delicious but hard work. His fingers burned from cracking the chillie-infused shells and he was sweating profusely. Sam paid no notice. Other customers stared at Tusker though. When he made eye contact, they would smile and nod.

They exited the cafe and started back towards Ahmed's shop. Tusker paused to peer into shops at the odds and ends for sale: a plastic jar full of broken wristwatches, rubber slippers, hair oil, wedding dresses, hijabs. As if to put a point on Sam's lunch explanation, he heard a voice coming through a speaker. They both turned to see a Toyota pickup truck with its windscreen ringed with white flowers drive slowly up the main road followed by two lines of Buddhist monks in robes. Behind them, a small crowd of men followed them, some carrying signs written in Sinhala. A man standing in the bed of the pickup was saying something into a megaphone and people on the sides of the road stopped and watched. Although Tusker couldn't understand what was being said, he sensed a tension in the air.

"Speak of the Devil," Sam said to him quietly. One of the signs being carried had a photograph of a monk with a large smooth head and no eyebrows. "That's Dhammasara, the current head of the BBH movement. He's based in Kandy and is almost never seen, but his followers hold these rallies all over the country. It's a sort of warning to the Muslims that they're everywhere."

Tusker nodded. "Charming."

The procession turned left at the roundabout and gradually moved out of sight. Tusker and Sam walked down the lane towards Majeed Motor Repairs. The sun had started to slide down in the West. They had a long drive ahead of them to Trincomalee. In front of the shop, Ahmed was wiping his hands with a rag. He grinned benevolently and handed the keys to Sam.

"Good timing. All finished." He thumbed towards the Land Rover. "The diff was full of twisted metal. Got a new one in there now. Well, new to you. It came out of this old one I'm rebuilding but should be good for another few years, as long as you keep fresh oil in it." He wagged his finger at Sam. "Also, fresh fluids all around, but I didn't have time to check your swivels. Keep an eye on those and bring it back soon."

"So grateful, Ahmed," Sam said, giving him a discreet peck on the cheek. The man smiled and looked at his feet. "How much can I pay you?" She pulled out a battered wallet and started thumbing rupees.

"Let's settle up another time, Samanthi," he said. "I needed the practice anyway and the parts were used."

Sam pressed a wad into his greasy hand and clutched it there. He smiled and muttered a thanks.

"Oh, did you check the air conditioning in this thing?" Tusker broke in. "It hasn't been working too well lately."

Sam and Ahmed laughed in unison. "Just tell her to drive a little faster," Ahmed said. "That's your A/C."

They climbed into the truck and Sam pulled the choke and turned the key. It rumbled to life. "Take good care, my friend," Sam called as she made a U-turn in the road. Ahmed just raised his hand in a wave and smiled. To Tusker, it looked like a sad smile.

Trinco

Trincomalee, Sri Lanka.
That evening.

The naval base in Trincomalee overlooks the crescent of water once called "the finest natural harbor in the world" by Winston Churchill. The blocks of administrative buildings and rows of barracks date back to the days of British rule in Sri Lanka, when Trinco was a strategic outpost for the Royal Navy. During World War II, the water here would have been thick with battle cruisers, destroyers, and minesweepers. It was also the last port of call for HMAS *Vampire*.

Today, Trincomalee harbor sees a small fleet of Sri Lankan Navy vessels, almost hidden at their moorings behind the bristling mass of fishing boats, passenger ferries and freighters from all corners of the globe. Sam navigated the Land Rover through the crowded, ancient roads around the perimeter of the harbor and finally turned up a steep drive and through an imposing gate that bore garish gold lettering in Sinhala, Tamil, and English. The latter read, "Sri Lankan Navy, Trincomalee Base."

They emerged from the tree-lined road onto the crest of the hill. Beyond the cream-colored colonial-era buildings was an impressive view of the Indian Ocean; in the other direction, the harbor lay below. Sam parked the Land Rover at what looked like the headquarters.

"Samanthi! Mr. Tusk!" Sebastian's shouts stirred them from their thoughts. Sebastian was jogging across the gravel drive towards the Land Rover, a huge smile on his face. Behind him was an older man in uniform, also smiling. It was Captain Fonseka, Sebastian's old friend and commander of the base. Sam and Tusker climbed down from the truck just in time to be hugged awkwardly by Sebastian.

"I was so worried... We searched..." He could barely contain himself, trying to get the words out. Sam reassuringly took his arm, trying to calm him.

"And to think, after being lost at sea, it was your old Landy that almost killed us in the end," she said with a laugh. "The important thing is, we're home and dry. But I'm dying for a cuppa. Any chance, Uncle?" Her eyes twinkled at the navy man.

"Of course, Samanthi." He grinned and spun on his heel to head back towards the office. "And you must be the archaeologist Sebastian was telling me about." He glanced sideways at Tusker as they walked. Tusker nodded and shook his hand. "I don't know whether you're brave or stupid to dive the *Vampire* on scuba." Though he frowned, his eyes were kind and his manner avuncular. Tusker liked him already.

Captain Fonseka's office was not air conditioned, but

a ceiling fan kept the air moving. The place seemed unchanged since British times, with heavy, dark wood furniture, yellowed photos on the wall, and dark green metal filing cabinets that were rusting at the corners from the humidity. A young woman in a smart skirted uniform entered the office with a tray of tea and Marie biscuits and set it on the desk, then quickly and silently left.

"So you say the anchor line was cut?" Sebastian scowled incredulously.

"Well, it sure looked that way," Tusker replied. "Naturally, I assumed it was an accident and the line had rubbed through on the gunwale or something, but now I don't know."

"I make sure to replace anchor lines regularly, and Roland would know to run it through a cleat," Sebastian said. He himself was a former navy man and ran a tight ship at the Deep Blue. He shook his head.

"Well, there's only one person who can tell us what happened, and that's Roland," said Sam. "We saw him on our way up here, in Pasikudah. He was with another man, a *suddha*... sorry, a white man—tall, silver haired—in a swank Land Cruiser. Rausing is his name. Tusker has met him."

"I managed to take a photo," Tusker said. He set down his cup and fished his phone from his cargo shorts. "Here it is. Sorry, it's a bit blurry. We were in a hurry to get out of there."

He handed the phone across the desk to Captain Fonseka, who pinched the screen to zoom in and studied it for a moment, then handed it back across.

"Yes, that's Rausing all right, the chap who's managing the harbor diving project in Batticaloa," he said matter of factly. "Nice enough gent, if a little odd." He took a bite of his biscuit, then wiped crumbs from his uniform. "Doesn't say much. I've only met him a few times, at the planning meetings for the project. We're providing security at the harbor."

"He owns the dive support vessel *Depth Charge*," Fonseka continued. "His company was contracted to handle the diving end of the harbor dig. Laying cable and such."

It was all making sense now, thought Tusker. The dead diver inside the *Vampire*, the sinking of the *Taprobane*, Roland disappearing.

"You think Rausing is somehow behind your diving accident?" The captain looked over the rim of his cup as he took a pull on his tea.

Tusker hesitated. Could Fonseka be trusted? He guessed he could, and proceeded to fill him in on the story so far—their dive to the *Vampire*, the bomb, the rescue by the fisherman, the hole in the *Taprobane's* hull, the helmet, the ROV footage and the stolen laptop.

Fonseka shook his head in disbelief and sat in silence for a full minute before he spoke. "I can't offer divers for a bomb disposal, I'm afraid," the commander said quietly.

"We don't do much of any mixed-gas diving here."

Tusker nodded. "I understand completely, sir. A hundred meters is the outside edge of what's safe for anyone on scuba."

"What I can offer is surface support, and a boarding party for the *Depth Charge*," Fonseka continued. "They are in our territorial waters, conducting a known act of terrorism on a war grave. Our commando team is in Colombo at the moment, but I can have them here the day after tomorrow."

"Two days' time will be too late. And what if Rausing has connections inside the government?" Tusker fondled the handle of his empty tea cup. He cleared his throat and looked around the desk at Fonseka, Sebastian, and finally, Sam.

"What I propose is that I do the dive myself. And I have one favor to ask of you, Captain. It may require a visit to your armory."

Looking for a Ship

Bay of Bengal, eight nautical miles east of Batticaloa.
The next night.

As soon as the faint glow coming from the otherwise dark
Depth Charge was visible, Sebastian eased back on the
throttle. They were counting on the dive vessel's crew not
seeing their small dinghy riding amidst the dark swells a
hundred yards astern.

"Take a bearing on that ship and then swim towards it at
around ten feet deep before descending to the wreck. Sam
will swim with your two deco cylinders and hand them
off to you." Sebastian was whispering, taking no chances.

They'd hatched this plan back at the naval base with
Commander Fonseka, after Tusker announced his
intentions to do the dive alone. Now, in the black night,
with a looming adversary and a long swim, Tusker was
second-guessing it.

"Right. Let's get on with it then," he said coldly, pulling
on his fins.

Sam had pleaded with him to let her come along but
Tusker insisted it would be easier to do this by himself.

He knew that if she was along and anything went wrong, the distraction of worrying about her would keep him from doing the job. But that's not what he'd told her. *"One can dive stealthier than two…"*

He wore a six-millimeter hooded wetsuit that Sebastian had pulled out of the back of his workshop. The suit was badly worn and frayed at the cuffs, but would keep him warmer at depth. He shivered, remembering his last freezing decompression. The thicker suit meant more buoyancy, which required more weight to descend. Tusker leaned forward, bracing his feet wide in the tossing skiff, and cinched a belt of lead weights around his waist. Sebastian and Sam helped him don the double tanks and a small "travel" bottle of air from which he could breathe for the swim and the descent. He strained under the additional 150 pounds of weight.

Sebastian opened a large black Pelican case in the bottom of the boat and carefully lifted out the limpet mine, a Russian-made *Ulitka* model, that Fonseka had gotten from the naval base's armory for Tusker the night before. Sebastian handed the unwieldy device to Tusker, who clipped it to two D-rings on his harness with carabiners. The skiff listed dangerously to one side as he sat on the gunwale. Sam and Sebastian countered it by hiking out opposite him.

"I'll splash in and wait for you, Sam," Tusker said. He spat in his mask, wiped and rinsed it, strapped it over his hood, and tumbled into the water. The splash sounded loud. Sebastian looked warily at the black silhouette of the *Depth Charge* in the distance. Sam quickly shouldered her single cylinder and rolled off the other side of the boat. Sebastian handed the deco cylinders over the side to her, one by one, and she clipped them to her own harness.

Tusker was bobbing alongside the skiff, holding himself away with a hand on its hull. Sam swam around to him. They looked into each other's eyes in the gloom. Tusker wanted to say something meaningful to her. This would be the last time they'd speak until after he would surface. *If* he would surface. But before he could open his mouth, Sebastian leaned over the side and whispered loudly to them.

"Get going!" he hissed. "Samanthi, I'll look out for you when you surface. Julian, we'll motor in just offshore and keep an eye out for your signal when you surface in a few hours. Remember, three pulses with your torch towards shore every 60 seconds."

Tusker nodded and clamped his mouthpiece between his teeth. He swiveled around towards the open sea and held up his wrist compass. Aligning the bezel so that North was on the swinging needle, he took a bearing on the approximate position of the *Depth Charge*. 50 degrees, give or take. If he could get close, he'd know when the big ship was above him. He caught Sam's eyes and gave her a wink. Then, a thumbs-down gesture. Time to go under and swim.

Tusker and Sam vented air from their buoyancy wings and their heads disappeared under the inky surface. He felt her hand on his arm. He switched on his torch and quickly held it tight against his compass and then his watch for a few seconds, then turned it off. The compass and watch dials glowed brightly, their luminescent markings excited from the burst of LED light. Then, with his left arm held at a right angle in front of him, he swam on the 50-degree bearing with slow, deliberate kicks. At this shallow depth, it was difficult going, and the swells pushed him and Sam up and down, their backs almost breaking the surface. The heavy mine attached to Tusker's chest made swimming awkward.

They swam in unison, Sam's hand held lightly on Tusker's arm. In the pitch black, Tusker felt an eerie sense of disembodiment. Sam's light touch through the neoprene provided a small measure of comfort. He remembered her fingers on his skin in that dark room back in Pottuvil and wished they were there now. Tusker only took his eyes off of the compass to check the time on his watch, counting off his swim distance. He could swim about 100 yards in 10 minutes. They must be getting close to the ship.

Sure enough, ahead he could sense something big in the water, a change in the sound: A low murmuring and a slapping of water, the hum of the ship's dynamic positioning system thrusters. At their shallow depth, if they got too close, they would swim right into the ship. A slight glow emanated down into the water column, light leaking through the moon pool, no doubt. It was time for Sam to leave him.

Tusker stopped swimming and turned to face her in the dark water, being careful to stay below the surface. They'd gone over the tank handoff several times. She'd have the 100 percent O$_2$ clipped on her right side. "Rich on the right," he remembered from his old tech diving instructor in Michigan. He reached out and, with his fingers, found the double-ended dog clip on her harness and unclipped it, being careful not to lose his grip. One mistake here—a dropped tank, a mixup of the two deco bottles—and they'd have to abort, or worse, he would die breathing the wrong gas at the wrong depth. He transferred the oxygen cylinder to his own right side and clipped it to the D-rings on his shoulder strap and hip belt. Then he did the same with the 50 percent nitrox tank, moving it from Sam's left to his own. The transfer of weight caused him to sink in the water and Sam to rise, but they'd accounted for this and she deflated her own wing while he moved the tanks. He momentarily gripped her on both forearms and squeezed a goodbye, hoping the gesture would convey all he wanted to say. She squeezed back. Then she was gone.

Tusker turned back to face the ship that loomed in front of him, invisible in the water. The other invisible ship, the HMAS *Vampire*, would be directly below him now, 350 feet down. Sebastian had pumped up the little 15-cubic-foot travel bottle as much as he could, but Tusker had breathed off of it for the ten-minute swim and needed it for the descent as well. He would discard it when he got to the wreck. There was no time to waste. He deflated his wing and sank like a stone, equalizing his ears every few feet. After three minutes, he quickly switched mouthpieces. He was now breathing off of his precious bottom gas mix. The clock was ticking.

Without an anchor line, and in complete darkness, he had

no sense of where he would touch bottom. A few feet off
and he'd descend right over the lip of the trench and keep
going into 2,000 feet of water. He blindly fumbled for
the backlight button on his dive computer and pressed
it. The display showed 300 feet and dropping. He had to
be getting close. Would he sense the *Vampire* as he did the
Depth Charge?

Tusker was dropping faster now, any buoyancy he had
higher up long gone. The ocean was reeling him in. He
inflated his wing with what seemed like a lot of air, and
his descent finally slowed. He was deep enough now
that it would be safe to switch on his torch. As he did,
something big flashed just in front of him and then was
gone. He felt a pulse of current from its thrust. A big fish?
A whale? A giant squid ascending after dark to feed? He
cast the beam of his torch around in wide arcs. Nothing.
Did he imagine it? Never mind the wildlife. Time to find
that shipwreck. Tusker was both glad and worried to see
the sea floor below him. He hadn't overshot and ended
up in the abyss, but the moonscape of the bottom also
meant he'd missed the wreck.

He checked the heading on his compass. He had no idea
in which direction the *Vampire* lay, so he would have
to swim big patterns until he found the ship: off in one
direction for 20 seconds, then a right-angle turn, then
swim another 20 seconds and so on until he'd returned to
his starting point. He'd increase his swim times and do
the same pattern until he bumped into the wreck.

On his third turn, something in the torch beam caught
his eye. On the sea floor, what looked like a box. Tusker

swam over and examined it. It was an ammunition box, and next to it, some .50-caliber shells lay strewn on the silty bottom. The ship had to be close by. He swung the torch beam around and saw something else in the distance, reflecting back the light. It looked huge and silver.

Tusker swam slowly in the direction of this shimmering object. It got brighter as he got closer and seemed to be moving, rippling. Then, when he was almost on top of it, it exploded into a thousand pieces. It had been a swirling school of silver amberjacks, swimming in a choreographed vortex. They'd scattered. He shook his head, groggy from the depth and rattled by this apparition. Now he'd have to resume his swimming pattern. He had to find that wreck, but his bottom gas would only last 40 minutes and he'd used up four on his search.

As he turned to start swimming, he brushed against something. A wall of coral, rising up from the bottom. And—yes—a perfect circle. A porthole. He'd found the *Vampire*.

Terminal Depth

On board the DSV Depth Charge.
30 minutes earlier.

Malcolm Rausing emerged from his stateroom aboard the
Depth Charge, locked the door, and descended the stairs
to the dive deck. On the steel staircase overlooking the
moon pool, he paused. It was pitch black aboard the ship,
as he'd ordered, but he could hear the clanking of metal
and the low chatter of men working below, readying
the hoist and diving bell. The air was moist and smelled
of the sea. The ship rolled heavily on big swells. These
weren't ideal conditions for diving, but Rausing couldn't
wait any longer.

Murray and Aitkens had been waiting in the hyperbaric
chamber for three days since their first dive to the *Vampire*,
remaining in saturation at an effective 350 feet of pressure
until their second attempt to salvage the bomb. They
passed the time watching porn on the internet, reading,
and sleeping. McElroy's personal effects lay in a heap on
his bunk, a constant reminder of his horrific fate, but the
two divers didn't dare speak of him. They'd be diving
without a third, a bell man. It would be risky, but then
everything about this project was.

"Keep yer feckin' dirty clothes on yer bunk, will ya?" Murray threw a pair of thermals at Aitkens, who laughed. The two men had known each other for years, having dived together out of Aberdeen in the '90s. It was Murray who'd coaxed Aitkens out of retirement for this "easy money" job in Sri Lanka, and the two men intended to treat it like a tropical holiday. They'd already planned to fly to the Maldives the next week with their newfound wealth.

"Prepare to transfer to the bell," came the disembodied voice from Dive Control. Murray nodded up at the camera in the corner of the room. The two men moved to the ladder and climbed up to the pressure hatch in the ceiling.

"Equalized. Transfer to the bell." Aitkens climbed the ladder, spun open the lock and pushed the hatch up into the diving bell. It was hot and muggy inside, and the two Scottish divers' faces shone with sweat. Murray closed the hatch with a thud and spun the lock shut. They sat down on the metal benches surrounding the hatch, which would be their exit to the sea, while the hoist slowly began to lift them off of the pressure chamber. The men braced themselves as the bell swung free and rocked lightly. Like astronauts in a crude capsule, they were about to be sent into an alien and hostile environment.

"Good dive, gentlemen," came Dive Control's voice. Then Rausing's voice.

"The cargo should be close to the hatch, with the lift bags still attached," he said coldly. "Bring the hoist over to the opening so you can secure it close to the wreck."

"Piece of cake, skipper," Murray replied. "Like hooking a dead fish." His joke was met with silence.

"Tell that to McElroy when you see him," Rausing finally said, then clicked off.

Murray shuddered at the thought of the dead man inside the *Vampire*, whose sopified body they'd no doubt encounter in a few minutes. He'd done body recoveries before, and seen plenty of corpses, but not that of anyone in whose death he'd taken an active part.

The bell splashed into the moonpool, where, despite being protected from the open ocean, it rode the up-and-down of the night's big swells. In a few moments, the bell was lowered into the depths and there was no sensation of movement at all. Only the depth gauge on the wall showed their progress to the sea floor. 150 feet, 200, 250, 300, then finally stopping at 330 fsw, "feet seawater." It was silent. The men were no longer sweating. The cooler temperature at depth chilled the bell, and the cold sweat on Murray's neck made him shiver.

"Terminal depth. Divers, prepare to exit the bell," came the instruction from Dive Control.

When both divers had their helmets secured, tool harnesses buckled on, and umbilicals connected, Murray bent and unscrewed the hatch in the floor of the bell. He felt the familiar moment of uncertainty: if the pressure was not equalized, the seawater would pour in and fill up the bell in seconds. But the pressure was right and, like it always did, the ocean lapped at the platform like a hotel kiddie pool. Strong flood lights illuminated the water below, but beyond the white arc, the sea was black. Small fish flitted in the pool of light, like insects drawn to a lantern.

Aitkens was the first to descend the ladder, his multi-colored umbilical trailing behind him, unspooling from its rack inside the bell. He dropped into the blackness. Murray, whose role on the previous dive was to remain as bell man, followed him out. Leaving an empty bell was against ordinary protocols of diving safety. But this was anything but ordinary diving.

The divers dropped 15 feet and landed feet-first on the silty bottom. "Divers on the bottom," Aitkens dutifully reported to Dive Control.

The *Vampire's* sloping hull rose directly in front of them. Murray glanced at Aitkens and gestured for him to stay put, then took two big, low gravity strides and vaulted onto the edge of the gash in the steel hull and dropped inside the bowels of the ship.

Deep Despair

350 feet beneath the Indian Ocean.
The same night.

Unlike his first dive on the *Vampire*, Tusker had managed
to arrive amidships instead of at the bow. This would
make his swim aft much shorter—good thing, because
he needed to save breathing gas. The current was lighter
tonight. Maybe his luck was changing. He'd shed his
small travel bottle and was now breathing off of his
helium bottom mix in his twin tanks. As he swam further
he could see the big Bofors gun on the port deck, still
pointing up at the surface in vain. It had been last fired 75
years ago at a swarm of Japanese fighter-bombers.

Ahead of him he caught a flash of light, then another.
He instinctively switched off his torch and stopped
swimming. *At night a candle's brighter than the sun,* he
thought, hoping they hadn't seen him, even at a distance.
It was so dark that he couldn't see his own hands, only
hear his gurgling breath, which roared in his ears. Two
pinpricks of bright white light dropped from an eerie
overhead floodlight. The diving bell of the *Depth Charge*.
They'd put divers in the water already. Tusker had hoped
he'd get there first. So much for changed luck.

Tusker collected himself and clamped his teeth around the mouthpiece. He'd have the element of surprise at least, and be slightly more mobile as a free swimmer than the tethered divers in their helmets and bulky suits. But he was outnumbered, and they had an unlimited supply of breathing gas, a luxury he didn't have.

Using the glow of the bell and the headlamps of the divers as a guide, he slowly finned forward, hoping the bright finish of his steel tanks didn't catch a reflection. He saw one diver, with his back to him, dragging a massive hoist hook along the sea bottom. The second diver was nowhere to be seen, but Tusker saw a glow coming from inside the hull. Yes, he'd gone in to fetch the bomb. They were planning to raise it with the hoist.

Tusker felt for the *Vampire's* hull in the dark and followed it down with his hand until he felt where it curved under, near the sea floor. He unclipped the heavy limpet mine from his harness and set it on the sand under the overhanging edge of the hull. He'd come back for it later. He needed to deal with these divers first. Fonseka had showed him how to use the mine back in Trinco and Tusker hoped he could remember.

Slowly, he swam up behind the first diver. He didn't relish the thought of killing but there was no time to consider the ethics. These men were here to steal a weapon of mass destruction and he had to stop them. He reached for the dive knife strapped to the inside of his right calf, a Wenoka Blackie Collins he kept razor sharp. It was a bigger knife than was the fashion with divers these days, a so called "pig sticker," but he was glad for it as he eyed the twisted cabling and hoses of the umbilical, thick as a man's wrist.

Tusker frog kicked to within ten feet of the other diver, then with two quick flutter kicks, he closed the remaining distance quickly. Just before he reached the diver, the man sensed Tusker, perhaps heard his breathing, and turned. He ducked and Tusker slashed, his movements slowed by the water, and missed with the knife. Now he was off balance, his quiver of deco bottles making quick movements awkward. Everything seemed to happen in slow motion, like a fight performed in treacle. Now they were both standing on the bottom, facing each other, Tusker in his fins with a quiver of heavy bottles hanging off of him, and the other man with his oversized helmet and plume of umbilicals trailing off into the darkness.

Tusker had to kill him quickly, before he could alert others on his radio. He lunged at the man's legs and tackled him around the ankles like a football linebacker. The diver tumbled in slow motion, the beam of his headlamps casting upward. *Now!* Tusker regained his own balance and slashed at the umbilical. He felt his knife purchase, but only nicked a cable, which frayed and unspooled. Nothing that would kill the man, but it must have been electrical: the torch on the helmet went dark. He hoped it had cut the diver's camera and radio feed too.

The eerie ambient light from the diving bell above lit the scene on the sea floor like a minimalist Greek tragedy, an armored warrior grappling with a minotaur on a naked stage. The other diver was on his knees now. Tusker felt a rush of water and saw the man's arm rise and fall. He felt a thud on the side of his head and reeled back, dazed. The diver had switched on a backup battery-powered torch on his helmet and Tusker could see the light cutting through a cloud of silt. The diver raised his arm again. He was holding a pry bar. This time, Tusker dodged the blow, which struck the sand harmlessly.

Tusker reached out with his right hand and grasped the umbilical. The diver shook his head like a dog in a tug of war but Tusker had got behind him and stayed there, matching his frantic twists and pivots. He brought the big knife up and sawed it through the umbilical and then the hose to his bailout bottle. There was a torrent of high pressure gas. He let go and watched as the diver weaved drunkenly along the sea floor, clutching the valves on his helmet, vainly trying to regain some breathing gas. Tusker could hear him grunting away the little gas remaining in his helmet, his torch light dancing crazily as he stumbled away. Tusker watched him fall to his knees and, with one hand, reach out to Tusker. Then, the diver slowly fell over onto the sea bed with a puff of silt, writhed briefly, then stopped moving. Tusker felt his gut wrench momentarily, then turned away.

The loss of diver comms and pressure would alert Dive Control aboard the *Depth Charge* and, no doubt, the second diver inside the wreck. There was no time to wait. Tusker had to move, fast.

The wreck loomed like a dead whale carcass, lying on its side with its long shadows of debris and coral dancing and swaying. Tusker caught his breath and took a second to check his pressure gauge. He was already past the first third of his bottom gas. He should be turning around now, but there was no point in dwelling on this. He was committed. He remembered the tight quarters inside the hull from his first dive here and quickly unclipped his decompression bottles from his harness and laid them down on the sand.

With three kicks, he lifted off the sea bed and was at the opening in the hull of the *Vampire*. The light inside was gone now: absolute darkness. He could hear the gurgle of a hard-hat diver's gas supply somewhere beneath him. Someone was waiting for him to enter. Tusker fumbled for his torch and switched it on, quickly swinging its beam back and forth inside the black hole. Suddenly, from his right, just inside the wreck, a hand reached out and ripped the mouthpiece from between his teeth. He took in a gulp of seawater and swung his arm instinctively. The torch fell from his hand and dangled from its tether on his wrist, its beam bouncing wildly around in the darkness. With his left hand, Tusker took his second regulator, which hung on a rubber strap close around his neck, and pushed it into his mouth, coughing into it. He still couldn't see the other diver but felt his presence close by.

Instinctively, Tusker ducked low and pushed off the inside of the hull, going deeper into the hold. As he did, he brushed past what he was sure was the other diver, caught his torch and swung it around. It was the dead naked body he'd seen on his first dive, now bloated and pale, floating freely around the confined space. The man's features were unrecognizable now. The eyes had been eaten by something and the flesh was already soft and pocked with bite marks. Tusker wretched and pushed the body away, his hand sinking into the flesh of the stomach. Where was the other diver?

Then he saw him. A large man in a black dive suit was moving towards him, pulling hand over hand on some overhead pipes on the bulkhead. His lack of fins made him awkward and his feet pedaled uselessly against the water. But he was gaining ground on Tusker. A large knife flashed in his right hand. Tusker saw the man's eyes behind the faceplate of the yellow Kirby-Morgan helmet. He gritted his teeth on his mouthpiece and kicked hard with his fins. The two men met in an awkward underwater dance, both of them thrashing, grabbing, and slashing. Their violence kicked up clouds of silt that hung suspended in the water, causing a complete whiteout.

Tusker's mask was a foot from the other diver's helmet and the two men made eye contact. Tusker dropped his torch and, with two hands, grasped the helmet on both sides and twisted, as if trying to unscrew the other man's head from his body. The diver lurched away into the cloud, vanishing for a moment. Tusker regained his buoyancy and shone his torch around, but it was like using high-beam headlamps in a blizzard. Behind him he felt a tug, then heard a roar. He couldn't breathe! His regulator hose had been cut and his double tanks were draining precious gas in a torrent of bubbles. Tusker again switched regulators, but he had to quickly shut off the valve of the severed hose or lose his gas. He reached back behind his head, feeling for the large knurled knob. In the dark, he was drifting down. Or was it up? He crashed into something hard and pinballed away from it, still fumbling for the valve. Finally, he found it and turned it one agonizing revolution at a time until the gushing became a hiss, then stopped.

How much gas had he lost? He didn't have time to check his gauge. He regained control of his dangling torch and cast it around the space. He'd drifted up and was pinned against the top of the wreck, which was actually the inside of the starboard hull of the capsized ship. Far below, he saw the beam of the diver's helmet torch through the silt. He was working at the bomb, filling one of the lift bags attached to it. It would be risky to try to swim down and stop him. He would be nearly out of breathing gas now. There was no doubt that Rausing knew what was happening, given the video feed.

Tusker glanced down at his wrist. The Aquastar was gone. It must have been torn from his wrist in the struggle with the *Depth Charge* diver. The watch he'd worn on every dive he'd done since age nine was now ticking away somewhere in the bowels of the wreck. Tusker didn't have time to curse. He had to stop the bomb, even if it meant breathing down his tanks to nothing. *There's only one way back to the surface now anyway.*

Consigned to the Depths

350 feet beneath the Indian Ocean.
The same night.

In the bottom of the bomb room, Murray caught his breath after his struggle with the scuba diver. Amidst the settling silt, he inflated the two massive lift bags that were slung on the bomb, left on their first dive by McElroy, whose bloated body floated somewhere above. Murray slowly inched the now-buoyant cargo towards the opening in the wreck. It was awkward going in the cramped confines of the cluttered room, made harder by the almost zero visibility. Once outside, he would hook it to the hoist dropped from the *Depth Charge*, which lay on the sea floor. Dive Control had already told him that Aitkens had been "incapacitated." *I better get double pay for this.*

He maneuvered toward the exit hole. Suddenly, out of the blackness, he was hit, hard, and knocked back into the wreck. The blow extinguished his head torch and he spun downwards in darkness, landing with a grunt on a pile of wooden crates that disintegrated into a cloud of dust on his impact.

Immediately, the other diver was on him, holding his helmet by the umbilical and shaking him. Murray struggled to gain his footing and clawed at the other man's mask. He managed to pull it sideways, flooding it and rendering him blind. Now was his chance. He pushed the flailing diver aside and used his umbilical to pull himself up the hull to the opening. Never mind the bomb. This was more than he'd signed up for.

Tusker straightened his mask and managed to clear the water by exhaling through his nose and lifting the bottom skirt. Nearly blinded from the salt and the silt, he swam towards the vague glow and saw a silhouette climbing up the inside of the hull. As he neared it, the bright yellow of the lift bag caught his eye. The bomb. It was floating near the exit, neutrally buoyant. Tusker swam up, up, up to Murray and, just as the big man reached the opening, grabbed a D-ring on the back of Murray's tool belt and pulled on it, hard. Murray lost his balance and teetered backwards. In a single, swift motion, Tusker clipped Murray's D-ring to the lift bag's carabiner and ripped the balloon's deflation cord.

Murray, suddenly attached to a 1,400-pound bulb of lead and uranium, fell off the hull like a stone and disappeared into the black hold of the *Vampire*, his helmet torch a wild, spinning beam. The tremendous weight and momentum sent him crashing through the remains of cargo, which fell on top of him, trapping him, weighted and buried in the 75-year old detritus of the dead British war machine. For a moment his umbilical was stretched taut, connecting Murray inside the wreck to the bell, and to the *Depth Charge* above. Then it gave way like a whip in a roar of bubbles.

Tusker turned away and found the cut in the hull outlined by the glow of the bell's flood lights. He kicked over to the opening. His breathing gas supply was near zero and the bailout bottles he'd stashed earlier were too rich a mixture for this depth. He had to get to the bell. As he exited the wreck he saw the heavy hook from the *Depth Charge*'s hoist lying on the muddy bottom. He swam cautiously towards the suspended bell. With his two divers dead and no bomb, why would Rausing bother to even hoist him to the surface, much less keep him under pressure long enough to decompress? He would have to negotiate. But what leverage did he have, alone and 350 feet deep? It would be just as easy for Rausing to flood the bell and kill him. No one would be the wiser.

Tusker crept up alongside the bell. He couldn't be sure what the gas mix was inside. But he had to take that chance. His pressure gauges were nearing zero. He climbed up into the bell and took the regulator out of his mouth. It was strange to suddenly be standing dry and breathing without a mouthpiece. He took a few cautious breaths. The helium mix in the bell was similar to what he'd been breathing in his tanks. A camera was suspended in the corner. There was nowhere to hide now. Everyone, including Rausing, knew he was in the bell.

As if in answer, a voice came over the intercom.

"You're out of options, Mr. Tusk." It was Rausing. He paused. "Except one."

"Go to hell," Tusker said, staring at the camera, his voice distorted by the helium.

"We have the girl," Rausing said, this time more sternly.

Sam! Was he bluffing? Tusker thought of her, swimming back to the skiff in the darkness after he descended. She could have easily been spotted, captured, maybe even killed already. And what about Sebastian?

"Bring me the bomb and then we can talk about your future." Rausing remained calm, a Human Resources manager talking to an employee.

"If you have her, put her on the radio," Tusker said. There was a long pause. Was Rausing stalling? Tusker considered his options. Think of Sam, do what Rausing asked and hope to foil their plans later, aboard the *Depth Charge*? He knew there was a slim possibility he'd be kept alive after a ride to the surface, much less hours of decompression aboard the ship. Rausing would no doubt find some creative and painful way to kill him. He loved Sam, but this was bigger than all of that. Much bigger. He had to return to the wreck and destroy the bomb, even if it killed him and Sam.

"Tusker?" Just as he'd made up his mind, Sam's voice came on the intercom. He closed his eyes, imagining her dark eyes, her glossy hair. "Tusker, look, I can take care of myself up here. You just finish what you started." She almost sounded cheery. "Besides, this asshole doesn't scare me." Then, a sharp noise, and silence. Tusker clenched his jaw. *Damn it!*

"Consider my offer, Mr. Tusk," Rausing's voice again. "Finish the job and we'll bring you to the surface. We'll lock Ms. de Silva in the hyperbaric chamber. You can join her there and decompress… together." There was a smirk in the voice.

Tusker looked around the bell for anything of use. There was a dive helmet, a cutting torch, some coiled umbilical. Nothing to aid in his escape. He had to cooperate. They had no doubt pressurized the chamber now, with Sam in it, effectively trapping her at the same depth as he was.

"My offer expires in ten seconds, Mr. Tusk," Rausing said, impatient. "Then we'll flood the bell and decompress the chamber with Ms. de Silva in it. Have you ever seen what happens to a body under rapid decompression, Mr. Tusk?"

The water below the hatch started to rise, bubbling into the bell. It swirled around his ankles. They had started decompressing the bell, allowing the sea to fill it up. He would either be decompressed too quickly, or drown. He wasn't sure which would happen first.

"You win, Rausing," he shouted. "I'll go hook the bomb."

"Wise decision, Mr. Tusk. Use the spare helmet attached to the Diver 3 umbilical. Secure it to the hoist and then return to the bell. Then we'll see you on board. And don't try anything stupid. We can see everything you do." The radio clicked off.

Tusker pulled the yellow helmet over his head and switched on the valve marked "Diver 3". With a hiss, breathing gas gushed into the helmet. He took a last look at the camera and stepped back into the dark sea.

The *Depth Charge*

Bay of Bengal, eight nautical miles east of Batticaloa.
The same night.

When Sam opened her eyes, she couldn't see anything.
Her scalp felt tender and damp. Even turning her head
resulted in such pain, she almost passed out.

Swimming back to the skiff where Thathi was waiting in
the dark, she'd been intercepted by a rubber boat with
a powerful outboard motor. Two men silently hauled
her aboard and threw her dive gear over the side. Before
she could even scream, one of the men hit her and
pulled a sack over her head. She felt the fast boat swing
crisply around and moaned helplessly as it bounced on
the swells back to the *Depth Charge*. Then, still blinded
by the sack, she was pushed up a metal staircase, two
decks above the water line. She heard shouts and more
footsteps approaching, and could feel the sway of the
ship on the swells and the sound of ocean spray.

One of the men who'd captured her roughly pulled the
sack off her head. She stood, squinting and dripping in
her wetsuit, on the dive deck. Then she saw a familiar
face: Roland's.

"I suppose yer wantin' a cup of tea now, eh?" He stood across from her, wearing Tusker's red Mount Gay Rum cap, his feet planted wide and his arms at his sides. He wore a large knife in a sheath at his hip, prominently displayed for her to see. "But first," he grinned and eyed her hungrily, "we should get you out of those wet clothes." He warily walked towards her, one hand on the knife's handle.

Sam remembered her own dive knife, in a leg sheath strapped over her wetsuit. It was a small, razor-sharp Spyderco she'd bought in Australia and always carried for cutting fishing nets. Her captors hadn't noticed it in the darkness. She tried to appear weak as Roland approached.

"I always wanted to see what you look like under that wetsuit, but had to play nice around yer daddy." He stepped closer and whispered, "Rausing can't expect us to not have a little fun now and then." The two men who'd brought her aboard stood a few feet behind Roland and looked at each other uncomfortably.

Roland was close enough that Sam could smell his sour nicotine breath. She let out an exaggerated groan and doubled over, as if in pain. "Get up!" hissed Roland.

In the same movement, she managed to pull the small blade from its sheath and conceal it in her palm. She stood up, facing Roland. Her head was pounding. Bending over had made her light headed. *Don't pass out now!*

Roland held up his knife. It was the same one he'd always

carried on the skiff and around the dive shop, corroded and probably dull. He poked its tip through the front of her wetsuit at her chest and slid the blade up, parting the neoprene. Up near the neck, where the rubber seal was thicker, the blade snagged and Roland used both hands to saw at the material. *Now!* Sam pivoted the tiny Spyderco in her hand so she gripped the hilt. In one motion, she grabbed the back of Roland's sweaty head with her free hand and punched the knife into his left eye. He screamed and fell away, clutching his face. Both knives hit the ship's steel decking with a clatter.

"Bitch!" Roland screamed.

Sam was already running. She'd been brought aboard forward of the moonpool, which was open to the sea. Sam could hear waves lapping deep within it and she briefly thought of jumping into it. But then she'd be trapped. She skirted the moon pool on the starboard side and when she reached the ship's railing, she looked both directions. To her right, she saw her two captors jogging towards her. Above them at the pilothouse railing was Rausing, glowering down at her with those pale eyes. Sam turned and continued running, finding herself suddenly on the open aft deck. Two men were busy maneuvering the hoist, which hung suspended from the crane over the moon pool. She sprinted past them.

"Stop her!" Rausing shouted from behind. Two more men, who were at the ship's aft hoist near the stern, registered what was happening and started after her. But she had a head start and was dodging the puddles of hydraulic fluid and coiled cable on her way to the back of the ship, where she assumed she'd find a motor skiff or dinghy tied up. When she reached the ship's stern, sure enough, a rubber boat was there, bobbing on the swells, tethered to a bollard, but only accessible from the next deck below.

Sam looked back. The two thugs from the pilothouse and the two men from the moon pool were now fanning out to surround her. It was at least a 25-foot drop to the Zodiac. If she landed on it, she'd break an ankle at the very least. It was no use. She turned to the men and held up her hands in surrender. Roland walked up behind them, clutching his eye socket, which was still pouring blood.

At least Thathi's not here, she thought. I can survive whatever they've got in store. She glanced around, making mental notes to plot a later escape. The shoreline twinkled to the west, miles away. A swim would be a long shot. It would have to be the rubber boat.

"And you must be the lovely Ms. de Silva." Rausing had walked up behind Roland, calmly. "I've half a mind to drop you where we found you, but with a little less…" He paused and a half smile crossed his face. "Buoyancy."

"But," he continued, "keeping you around a bit longer may prove useful."

A man wearing a headset microphone crossed the open deck of the boat and whispered in Rausing's ear. He cocked his head and thought for a moment, then turned his attention back to Sam.

"Well, well, speak of the Devil," he said, and motioned

to the two large men from the Zodiac to bring her and follow. "Go clean yourself up," he said coldly to Roland as they walked past. "And make sure she doesn't have any more weapons on her."

They ascended a metal staircase and stepped inside the compartment one level above the dive deck. It was some sort of control room, monitoring the divers below. The air conditioning was blowing frigid, and Sam shivered in her soaking wetsuit. On the video monitors, she could see the inside of a diving bell in high definition. *Tusker!* She could see him staring up at the camera. If he was in the bell, something was wrong, Sam thought.

"Tusker, look, I can take care of myself up here," she said to the image of Tusker on the video screen. "You just finish what you started."

Then, the threat, the exchange over the radio, and another crack on the skull. Sam crumpled to the room's steel floor.

"Throw Ms. de Silva in the chamber," Rausing said calmly. His pale eyes looked straight into Sam's soul. "Mr. Tusk will be joining you there shortly."

A Grisly Errand

350 feet beneath the Indian Ocean.

Tusker dropped like a stone to the sea floor and landed with a thud, a slow-motion puff of silt billowing up to engulf him. He was starting to shiver from the cold. He'd been in the water for close to an hour now, without the advantage of an umbilical hot water line. He gathered himself and waited for the cloud to settle before walking over towards the *Vampire*, which loomed like a dark mountain in front of him. The maw in the hull was directly above him, but Tusker knew that the limpet mine he'd hidden earlier was somewhere in the darkness just to his left. Rausing would be watching his every move from the helmet mounted camera. Somehow he had to get it without being seen. But how?

"Get moving." Rausing's voice came through clearly in his helmet. Tusker suddenly had an idea.

"I'm having trouble seeing," he answered back. "This head torch is aimed wrong or something." He reached up and made a show of fumbling with the head torch, covering it with his hand. The view in Dive Control would be blackness now. He twisted the torch hard until it faced straight up at a crazy angle and quickly kicked up a cloud of silt from the sea bottom.

"Stop fooling around, Tusk," Rausing's voice was raised. "Hook the bomb and get back to the bell or it'll be more than your girlfriend's ears that are popping."

Tusker scuffled his feet under the edge of the hull. Yes, there it was. The unmistakable turtle shell bulk of the mine. He squatted down, huffing into the microphone to exaggerate the sound of his effort. With one swift movement, he scooped up the mine, its carabiners still attached, and clipped it to his harness. It would be awkward going now, but he'd have to keep it out of sight of the camera. He twisted the torch back down and aimed it ahead, hoping the commotion and silt had kept Rausing from seeing.

Draped through the cut in the hull, now limp, was the umbilical torn from the diver trapped inside the wreck. Bubbles blossomed from the hole, catching the light from Tusker's torch before disappearing into the blackness above. He grimaced at the prospect of having to detach the awkward bomb from Murray's corpse.

"I'm going to take the hoist into the wreck and hook the bomb," Tusker said in a mechanical voice he hoped would sound confident. There was silence for a moment. Then Rausing replied.

"Use the lift bags to get it out. We can't risk the hoist fouling on the wreck."

"I can guide it out," Tusker replied authoritatively. "Your

217

man is part of the cargo now, and it will be too difficult for me to extricate the bomb from him and the debris." Silence again. No doubt Rausing was conferring with his crane operator.

"Fine, but make it fast."

Tusker lifted the hook off the sea floor. It was half his own height and incredibly heavy. He dragged it over to the wreck and managed to wrestle it up and into the opening. It dropped inside. He followed it in.

"OK, feed out some cable," he commanded. "I'm going to swim down to the bottom."

The cable slackened and Tusker guided the unwieldy hook down the length of the upturned cargo hold. The light of his torch illuminated the grisly scene at the bottom. Murray's torso was buried in debris, three of his limbs visible, a leg at an odd angle. And there, above the collar of his dive suit, was what was left of his head. It had been nearly torn clean off by the force of the taut umbilical on his helmet. Tusker averted his eyes, focusing on the task at hand.

He landed on the twisted metal remains of what looked like an old shelving unit next to Murray's corpse. He aimed his torch alongside and started to pull debris away to expose the bomb. He stopped every few seconds to settle the plumes of silt that clouded his view. Finally he saw a large fin. The rear end of the bomb. There was no way he could have fished this out with lift bags. He stepped back and found the hoist hook swaying behind him, called up for more slack, then clipped the hook to a lift ring on the bomb.

"OK, it's hooked," he said calmly. "Raise the hoist slowly. I'll tell you when to stop."

The heavy cable went taut and the bomb shifted slightly, sending debris cascading across the room and creating a whiteout. This could work to Tusker's advantage.

"Keep hoisting," he said. "Easy does it." The bomb continued to rise, with Murray's body grotesquely suspended from one of the lift rings and a limp yellow lift bag providing a garish bit of gift wrapping for the deck crew above. Just before the bomb started swinging free, Tusker inched close to it and unclipped the limpet mine from his harness. He clamped it onto the bomb's casing, its powerful magnets gripping like its namesake mollusk does on rocks. He couldn't very well look at the time fuse since it would appear on Rausing's video screen above, but he remembered Fonseka telling him that a full turn would be one hour before the *boom*. He gave it a half turn. That should buy him 30 minutes.

"OK, she's clear!" he shouted almost enthusiastically. "Pull it up and keep it slow."

The suspended bomb rose in the silty darkness. Tusker swam up next to it, guiding it towards the opening in the hull, careful not to show the limpet mine with his helmet camera.

Once clear of the wreck, Tusker swam clear and called

out. "It's outside the wreck. You can go ahead and raise it."

The bomb suddenly shot up past him. Then, to his horror, he saw the bell being raised as well. He should have expected as much. He reached up to his own umbilical and pulled hard, climbing hand over hand until he was ten feet below the bottom of the bell. He took a breath but got nothing. They'd shut off his gas. He flew up his tether, holding his breath now. The helmet started filling with cold seawater, blinding him. *Clang!* His helmet bashed into the bottom of the ladder. The bell! With one clean motion, Tusker hurled himself up the ladder into the bell, which was rocketing to the surface. He threw himself on the bell's floor, ripped off the helmet and cursed loudly.

"Good show, Mr. Tusk," came a bemused voice on the intercom. "I look forward to welcoming you on board the *Depth Charge.*"

Decompression Sickness

*On board the DSV Depth Charge, eight nautical miles
east of Batticaloa.
Ten minutes later.*

Through the tiny porthole in the diving bell, Tusker could
see the floodlit moon pool of the *Depth Charge*. Water
cascaded off the flanks of the bell as it swayed, suspended
above the ship's aft deck. Why should Rausing even
bother to keep him alive at this point? Why didn't he
flood the bell instead of hoisting him topside?

He squinted through the thick Perspex. Near the transom,
a hoist was spooling up the cable attached to the bomb.
Four men were laboring there, making sure it didn't
foul on the pulley as it came up. Would they keep him
suspended here until the bomb was unloaded? They
would surely see the limpet mine under the diver's
corpse and kill him and Sam immediately. How long until
the mine would explode? Another ten minutes? Fifteen?
And would it be enough to trigger the bomb? Either way,
Tusker had resigned himself to an agonizing and fast
death. His body had been absorbing breathing gas at ten
times the pressure at sea level for over an hour. He would
need days to decompress before safely emerging from a
bell or hyperbaric chamber. His only hope was to get Sam

221

off the ship before all hell broke loose. *But how?*

Finally, the bell started to move. It was swung out of the moon pool and lowered onto its trunk for passage into the ship's hyperbaric chamber. He guessed Rausing simply wanted to observe their gruesome death through rapid decompression. Sick bastard. At least death would come quickly.

The bell clunked onto the chamber's trunk and a green light in the bell flickered on. A sign next to it read *EQUALIZED*. Tusker stared at the sign for a moment. Then he cautiously bent over and gripped the locking wheel on the hatch in the floor of the bell, unconsciously holding his breath. *This could be it.* With a small hiss, the hatch unsealed and he spun the wheel until it was unlocked. He exhaled. He lifted it out of the way and shimmied down the ladder into the hyperbaric chamber. When he got the bottom and turned around, there was Sam.

"Boy, am I glad to see you!" she squealed, her voice altered by the helium they were breathing. She looked worn out, more tired than he'd ever seen her. There was a cut on her forehead and an egg-sized lump matted with blood at her hairline.

"I guess absence does make the heart grow fonder," Tusker said, managing a weak smile. They embraced. Tusker was still in his wetsuit and shivered in the chilled air. Sam felt warm and soft. He closed his eyes and tried not to think of their impending fate.

"I need to tell you something," Tusker said as he pulled away from Sam. "It's important." She searched his face. Just then, a familiar voice interrupted. Rausing. He was at the chamber hatch, his face filling the window. His large, pale eyes bored into Tusker.

"Mr. Tusk," he said, ignoring Sam. Speaking through an intercom made his voice sound even more disembodied. "You've done me a great service, retrieving my cargo and disposing of my overpriced hired help. Thank you." A thin smile.

"You should know that the Sri Lankan Navy is on its way out here right now," Tusker bluffed. "If you drop the bomb back in the sea and no harm comes to us, no one needs to know any of this happened." He was trying to seem reasonable but also firm.

Rausing looked down and chuckled. "Mr, Tusk, do you honestly think I could have gotten this far without thinking of every contingency? The navy, the police, they won't cause any problems for me. Your friend, Mr. Karuna, and his friends were but a mere inconvenience. Just as you have been."

Tusker stepped close to the thick glass and gritted his teeth. "You son of a bitch," he said, spitting the words out at Rausing.

Rausing ignored him. "We've not had a single accident onboard the *Depth Charge*," he continued, then twitched his head, recalling McElroy's misfortune. He cleared his throat. "So I've never been able to satisfy my curiosity about the effects of rapid decompression."

Here we go, thought Tusker. He reached over and gripped Sam's hand and stepped back into the chamber a few paces. "If you are going to kill us, get it over with, you sick bastard." Sam inhaled sharply and gripped Tusker's hand tightly.

Rausing smiled. "You seem worried, Mr. Tusk, but I thought we'd experiment with someone a little more... expendable, as a test, just to make sure we do it right." He nodded to someone down the corridor, out of sight of Tusker.

With that, there was a hiss from the adjoining chamber, one that would normally be used to insert new divers or medical staff in case treatment was needed. This chamber was separated from the main one, where Tusker and Sam were, by a thick pressure hatch. Through a porthole, Tusker saw a familiar face. Roland. He had a bandage over one eye and looked rough. He had been pushed in against his will by a muscular man with a shaved head and mustache.

"As you might guess, my little project here in Sri Lanka is like the chamber you find yourselves in. Even a tiny leak would be disastrous to it." He nodded in the direction of Roland in the adjoining chamber. "I've decided Mr. Van der Schyff may one day be a leak."

Tusker looked over at Roland, who was banging on the outer hatch of his chamber, shouting in Dutch. He paced around the chamber, squeezing his nose and crying in agony. Tusker knew what was going to happen. Rausing stepped back from the porthole and nodded to his left. There was a hiss. Tusker grabbed Sam and held his hand over her eyes. "Don't watch!" he whispered to her loudly. But Tusker couldn't look away.

There was a piercing scream, unlike anything human or animal that Tusker had ever heard. Then a loud pop. Then silence. Pink-tinged pulp covered the porthole to the adjoining chamber. Tusker closed his eyes before he could see it drip.

"Mercifully fast, wouldn't you say, Mr. Tusk?" Rausing was back on the intercom, peering in. His face was almost expressionless but there was something there—satisfaction? Pleasure? "Now, I regret to say, I fear that you and Ms. de Silva here may know too much as well. Like I said about leaks… Now which one of you will pop first?" He smiled.

Tusker felt his resolve and his energy drain away, sad that Rausing's face might be the last thing he would see, sad that he'd gotten Sam into this mess. *Where was that limpet mine?* He instinctively glanced at his wrist, then remembered his watch was gone. Had he set the mine incorrectly? It had to have been 30 minutes by now!

Rausing saw Tusker's gesture. *An odd moment to check the time…* Something dawned on him and he cocked his head. At that moment, a technician ran up behind Rausing.

"What is it?" Rausing hissed, visibly annoyed. The man whispered something in his ear. Rausing pulled back, confused, then looked in at Tusker. His eyes blazed. Behind him, a siren started to blare. Technicians were running past in the corridor. Rausing scowled and vanished from the porthole.

Tusker turned to Sam. "The limpet mine. I set it for 30 minutes and attached it to the bomb." Sam's eyes got big.

"But how do we..." she started. Tusker was already running across the chamber.

"Over here, quick!" he called to Sam. "It's a long shot, but our only one."

There was a small hatch at the top of a ladder in the corner of the chamber. A series of switches, lights and gauges glowed below it on the bulkhead, with a plaque that read, *SPHLB*. Tusker surveyed the bank of switches, then flipped on the one labeled *Equalize*. He watched the gauge's needle rise. When it neared ten atmospheres, it slowed and then stopped. A green light flashed on. He turned to Sam.

"Time to go," he said, and scampered up the ladder, spun a locking wheel on the hatch, and pushed the heavy door upward. Sam followed him and they emerged into a long horizontal cylinder with what looked like airplane seats facing each other. Rigged above were racks of flotation devices, Pelican cases and oxygen bottles. It was the ship's self-propelled hyperbaric lifeboat.

While a modern dive support vessel's crew can man ordinary lifeboats or be airlifted off the deck by a rescue helicopter, divers under pressure inside the hyperbaric chamber don't have any choice but to remain at "depth." The *Depth Charge's* hyperbaric lifeboat was sealed one deck above the pressure chamber by a vertical trunk and could be pressurized for an emergency escape. It was capable of supporting up to eight divers for up to two weeks, outfitted with its own emergency water and rations and separate, unpressurized cockpit which would ordinarily be manned by someone from the ship's non-diving crew.

Tusker slammed shut the hatch and spun the locking wheel tight, then began frantically searching the controls inside.

"How do we get off the ship?" Sam cried out.

"I'm not sure, but there must be some kind of explosive davit releases." Tusker said as he combed the ceiling and walls. "Found it!"

A large red knob, straight out of a cartoon, was situated on the forward bulkhead. A plaque next to it read, *RELEASE*. Tusker ran to it. "Sit down and strap in. This is going to be rough."

Sam threw herself into one of the bolstered chairs and strapped a safety harness on. Tusker braced himself and hit the red button with his fist. There was a loud, muffled explosion above their heads and then a moment of silence. They dropped like an elevator with a broken cable. Then the lifeboat slammed into the ocean.

Tusker was thrown up against the ceiling and then fell

hard across two chairs. He felt a rib, maybe two, crack, and howled in pain. The boat pitched wildly in the swells. It was shaped like a barrel and behaved like one in the open ocean. Tusker hoped for a brief second that they would drift far enough away from the *Depth Charge* before the bomb exploded.

As if in answer, a massive explosion blanketed the lifeboat in heat and light. The concussion was deafening and Tusker could feel the boat go airborne. Then he was tossed, first against the ceiling, then the floor, then the ceiling, then the floor again. Finally, mercifully, all went dark.

Blast Radius

Bay of Bengal, ten nautical miles east of Batticaloa.
Two hours later.

It was later reported that the white flash of the explosion could be seen as far away as Trincomalee. Minutes later, a five-foot wall of water pushed a quarter mile inland up and down the coast, causing a tsunami panic. But compared to the 2004 disaster, the waves subsided quickly and flooding was minimal. The story made the BBC and CNN later that day.

Rumors quickly spread: the Tamil Tigers were back. It was a Chinese submarine, an underwater volcano. In Colombo, President Halangoda was awakened by his private secretary to receive the news. He immediately knew what it was, but feigned surprise.

Ten miles out to sea, Tusker opened his eyes. His head was throbbing and he struggled to remember where he was. All he could see was a haze of orange. As he regained his senses, he realized he was buried under a pile of life jackets. He clawed his way out as if swimming until he recognized the sterile interior of the hyperbaric lifeboat. The rows of seats were still bolted to the floor, but everything else had been ripped from the walls, the storage compartments, and ceiling, and thrown around the cabin.

Tusker could hear a steady hum and the sloshing of water. He took a deep breath—and realized that if he still could, the lifeboat had not been breached by the blast. The boat was effectively a floating compression chamber, and they were still trapped at the equivalent of 350 feet of water pressure. But at least they were alive.

But what about Sam? Tusker swiveled around and saw her slumped in one of the seats. She'd fastened herself with the four-point safety harness as he'd told her to do. But was she alive?

Tusker waded through the piles of debris on the floor to her. He leaned in, with his ear next to her face, hoping to hear, or feel, a breath.

"Trying to take advantage of a vulnerable woman?"

Tusker pulled back with a grin. "Are you OK?" He clutched her face in both hands and studied her eyes.

"Sure," she replied. "I mean, I think so. I may have dozed off there."

"Well, thanks for caring about me!" Tusker shot back with a smile. "I was left for dead under a pile of life jackets!"

Sam laughed. She unclipped her harness and climbed over the seat back. There was a row of small portholes, each about half a foot thick against the hyperbaric pressure. She peered out.

"Come take a look at this!"

Tusker joined her at the windows and craned his neck to see out the next porthole. In the distance was an apocalyptic scene. A towering cloud of white vapor culminated in what looked like a massive thunderhead. At the surface of the water was a jumbled mass of indeterminate flotsam—remnants, he grimly thought, of the *Depth Charge*. Closer to the lifeboat was a raft of dead fish.

"I guess that bomb was for real," Sam said in a quiet voice, still peering out the window. "How did we manage to survive the blast?"

"I suspect the hull on this boat is really thick, since it has to contain the pressure," Tusker shrugged. "Thick enough to survive a bomb blast."

In fact, the lifeboat had been thrown almost one hundred yards by the force of the explosion. The self-righting lifeboat tossed like a cork, ripping loose everything inside. But the thick walls and high pressure inside resisted implosion. Only now, they were adrift.

"We'll just have to wait to be found, I suppose," Tusker said, aimlessly throwing debris into heaps in an attempt to tidy the cabin. "We have no way to pilot this thing."

Tusker and Sam were merely passengers. Even the emergency radio was in the boat's pilothouse, which was visible through the thick front porthole, but as inaccessible to them as the shore itself.

"It seems we're destined to always be lost at sea together," Sam said, smiling wearily.

"At least this time we have rations," Tusker replied, holding up a pair of packaged meals he'd found. "Now if we could only find the beer fridge."

Prevailing Winds

Bay of Bengal, eight nautical miles east of Batticaloa.
Later that day.

It had been 30 years since Sebastian de Silva had been on a naval vessel. Now he found himself pacing the decks of the SLNS *Samudra*, a patrol boat stationed out of Trincomalee, a pair of binoculars pressed to the goggles of his protective mask. He was sweating profusely inside a bright orange hazmat suit. He felt a gloved hand on his shoulder.

"We'll find them, *machang*," Captain Fonseka addressed him informally, though his reassurance was less than convincing. He was also wearing a hazmat suit, just like the rest of the crew who were scanning the water. Sebastian didn't lower the binoculars from his face. The scene was carnage: dead fish, a raft of debris.

"This must have been ground zero," he said grimly. "The radius of debris seems to spiral out from here."

"Yes, and the prevailing wind is offshore, which is good and bad," Fonseka replied. "The radiation cloud has blown to the east, but it also means so have Samanthi and Mr. Tusk, if..." he trailed off. "There's little point lingering in this area," he continued. "I'll direct the captain to get beyond the debris and we'll sweep arcs. I've also got helicopters coming to search from the air." He patted Sebastian's shoulder once more and then walked away.

Inside the hyperbaric lifeboat, Tusker had busied himself with tidying the cabin. He re-stowed the life jackets in their overhead racks, rehung the survival suits in their lockers, and stacked the remaining pile of waterproof cases in a corner. *If we're going to be in here for a few days, might as well.* Sam was asleep on one of the small bunks built into the wall of the lifeboat, mouth slightly open, snoring quietly. Tusker's gaze lingered on her face and tangled, loose braid and he smiled briefly.

With no means of driving or navigating the lifeboat, they were at the mercy of the currents and wind. At least we'll be able to safely decompress and have food and water for a few days, Tusker thought. Someone will find us.

He walked over to a starboard porthole and peered out. The view was distorted from the thick Perspex, but the air looked hazy, and to the west he could still see a dark cloud hovering high above the water. He wondered how much damage had been done. Had his plan caused more damage than good? He'd meant to use the limpet mine to destroy the bomb inside the *Vampire*, not on the surface. Had a wave flooded the coastline, killing thousands? And what about the radiation?

How long had they been drifting? He glanced at his wrist, then remembered his watch had been lost in the wreck. It made him think of his father, and of the day he had given him the Aquastar. It was on their cabin's dock at Lac La Belle in Michigan's Upper Peninsula. Tusker was nine and had just emerged from the water, struggling with the heavy scuba cylinder. His father, in his wheelchair, shouted encouragement. Looking back he realized that his father knew he was dying. The bends he'd sustained five years earlier had paralyzed him from the chest down. Worsening pneumonia had made it difficult for him to breathe. But he insisted that he would teach Tusker to dive, even if it meant doing it from the dock.

"Stay too long, too deep, and you'll end up like me." He smiled at young Julian. "You're going to need a good watch." He pressed the Aquastar into Tusker's palm.

Tusker felt a deep sadness looking at his empty wrist and wondered what his father would have thought of him now. He hoped he'd be proud of him.

Suddenly, he was jolted out of his thoughts by a loud *thwack-thwack*. He knew what it was immediately. A helicopter.

Fallout

Sri Lanka.
Six months later.

A month after the mysterious explosion, the coastline between Trinco and Batticaloa still stank from the dead fish drifting ashore. Debris was washing up as far south as Arugam Bay and a mutilated corpse was discovered in the lagoon at Pasikudah. Fishermen returned to harbor with empty holds and recreational diving was declared off limits by the marine authorities.

President Halangoda's opponents accused him of a cover up. Rumors of a secret deal with the Chinese swirled. The president deflected the criticism, suggesting an ISIS connection and even briefly jailing the mayor of Batticaloa. Ramadan was a subdued affair, with the minority celebrants wary of backlash and violence. After a brief delay and cleanup from the flooding, the harbor project resumed. A Chinese diving firm was brought in to finish the underwater work there.

Despite the turmoil, Halangoda easily won re-election, running on a nationalist anti-Muslim platform with the strong backing of the Sinhalese majority and the Buddhist Power Army. In the swearing in of the new government at Parliament, a traditional Buddhist blessing was given by the Venerable Udugala Dhammasara.

Sebastian de Silva closed down the Deep Blue Resort and headed back to Colombo to await the start of the west coast diving season. It promised to be a challenging one. Tourism was down and the southwest monsoon was running late this year.

Ahmed Raheem had had enough. He shuttered his garage in Pasikudah and made plans to move his family to Pakistan, where his brother assured him he could find work repairing farm equipment. Before he closed the heavy overhead door to his shop, he took a last look at the half-assembled old Land Rover inside, still on jack stands. He'd been restoring it for years, but it would be too expensive to ship. The new shop owner promised to finish the job. Ahmed hoped he would.

Ian Walsh stayed on in Sri Lanka, marrying a local woman and accepting Upali Karuna's old directorship at the Ministry of Culture, History and Archaeology. He had partially recovered from the bends and was able to walk with a cane, but he would likely never dive again. He still enjoyed being on boats and the tropical climate agreed with him.

In Galle, Raj, the fisherman, went back to his nightly work, plying the offshore reefs for mackerel, snapper, and the occasional shark. One day, while cleaning nets in his shed by the Galle harbor, he knocked over a bucket of dirty water. Something shiny spilled out and he picked it up. It was some sort of shackle from a sailing boat and engraved on its side was a symbol, three lines creating an arrow. He turned it over in his hands and studied it. Deciding it could be of no use to him, he stepped out of the shed and, with the perfect form of the street cricket bowler he once was, heaved it across the road, where it skipped once on the surface of the harbor and sank like a stone.

Mad Dogs and Michiganders

*Lac la Belle, Michigan's Upper Peninsula.
January.*

Dizzying, the stars and the cold. Tusker clipped out of
his skis halfway across the frozen lake and crunched
awkwardly in a drunken radius away from them in his
stiff boots, gazing upwards. He wanted to burn this
experience into his memory—the empty loneliness of
a billion winter stars, the deep snow, the sharp biting
air. He thought of Upali and how he hated the cold of a
Michigan winter. He laughed out loud. Sri Lanka seemed
a distant memory now—Rausing, Roland, the *Depth
Charge*, all of it.

It was Tusker's last night in the middle of nowhere.
Tomorrow he would return home, each mile of the
drive back spooling in the real world like one of the
lunker bass that slept in the lake below his feet. The
new semester started in a week, and with it, another
crop of students, more campus politics, papers to write,
the long slog into spring.

He snapped into the bindings again. The left one had
frozen up with compacted snow, and he had to remove a
glove to clear it. His fingers burned, and he shoved them

back into his glove. He forced his boot into the binding, snapping off a splinter of yellow plastic in the process. He couldn't be bothered now. As long as he could ski back to the cabin, he could deal with a new binding back home next week.

The cabin was cheerful from a distance. He'd stoked the fire before setting out, and from the smell of the smoke on the wind, he knew it would still be warm inside. He hurriedly took off the skis and leaned them up on the cabin's small porch, not bothering to wipe the icy buildup from them. As he stepped into the cabin, the warmth enveloped him. He stripped off his anorak, cap, and gloves, and tossed them in a heap on the bench inside the door.

"I was about to send out the search party." Samanthi de Silva smiled at him from across the single room. She was sitting on the floor near the fire, her knees pulled up to her chin. She wore one of Tusker's thick sweaters and her hair was pulled back, a few wisps trailing down around her face. The firelight made her skin glow.

"I need to teach you how to ski!" Tusker replied and pulled off his boots.

"Um, no thanks. I'm quite fine here by the fire." Sam held out a silver flask. "Take a pull, it'll warm you up."

Tusker took it from her and tipped it back into his mouth. The scotch was warm and smoky. He took another drink, then screwed down the cap.

"It's gotten colder outside," he said, sliding down next to Sam on the rug. She'd kept the fire fed with logs and it danced in the grate.

"I can tell!" she exclaimed. "Don't you dare come to me for warmth with your cold hands. Nobody made you go outside!" She mockingly pulled away from him. "You know the saying, 'Only mad dogs and Englishmen go out in the noon day sun?' Well, I think there must be one about crazy Americans and the midnight snow."

Tusker laughed and slid his cold hand under her sweater against her warm, bare stomach. She shrieked but didn't resist. He leaned in and kissed her hard, sliding his hand further up. Her mouth was warm and tasted of whisky.

"Get out of those wet clothes," she whispered, pulling at his wool undershirt. "You'll catch a chill." He peeled off the damp shirt, then his ski pants and sat there, exposed, in front of the fire, which snapped and fizzed. He was buzzed from the scotch and dazed with desire.

"Your turn," he said to Sam. This time, she said nothing but only met his gaze. She slowly got to her knees and pulled the sweater over her head. She wore nothing underneath. When she leaned close to him, he could hear her breathing. Her eyes were like black pools, and Tusker could see the fire reflected in them. He pulled her down. She gasped.

"See, winter's not so bad, is it?" he said quietly. As if for emphasis, the wind outside moaned in the pines. A log fell in the fireplace, sending up a shower of sparks.

She grinned. "As long as you have someone to keep you warm."

Epilogue

By the summer of 1942, the American atomic bomb program, known as the "Manhattan Project," had gained momentum, despite getting a later start than the British Tube Alloys program. The sheer might and resources of the United States quickly outstripped the efforts of its ally across the Atlantic. By early 1943, with secrecy considered paramount, information sharing had dried up almost entirely between the U.S. and the United Kingdom.

Sensing that his country's nuclear ambitions were slipping away, British prime minister Winston Churchill finally negotiated terms of collaboration with American President Franklin Roosevelt. Signed in August, 1943, the Quebec Agreement formalized the absorption of Tube Alloys into the Manhattan Project, with a promise of collaboration, both "industrial and commercial."

The agreement stated, "First, we will never use this agency against each other; secondly, we will not use it against third parties without each other's consent; and thirdly, we will not either of us communicate any information about Tube Alloys to third parties except by mutual consent."

On 9 August, 1945, at 8:15 local time, an American

bomber dropped an atomic bomb, nicknamed "Fat Man," on the Japanese city of Hiroshima. Three days later, a second bomb, called "Little Boy," was released over Nagasaki. They remain the only two nuclear weapons ever deployed in wartime. Japan formally surrendered shortly afterwards, ending World War II.

The HMAS *Vampire*, sunk by Japanese aerial attack on 9 April, 1942, has never officially been found.

Acknowledgements

A lot of people have the dream of writing a novel. I did for many years and, in fact, wrote about 50 pages of one ten years ago, only to abandon it. Even after a long career of writing everything from technical manuals to ad copy to wristwatch reviews, the prospect of sitting down and hammering out 60,000 words of a coherent, entertaining, and well-written story scared me. The fact is, it's a daunting task.

There are a few things that I've found separate the creation of a novel from other genres of writing. First of all, the sheer discipline and perseverance to face the blank page for an extended period. I've read that Alistair Maclean wrote his thrillers in about a month. Ian Fleming wrote one a year, spending three months in Jamaica writing, then flying back to London to edit. Rinse and repeat. That's not me. *Depth Charge* has taken 18 months, from first word to printing.

And then there's the research. Though only a handful of saturation and technical divers, Sri Lankan Buddhists, or British historians might read this book, I didn't want to get details wrong in any of those fields of expertise. Online research can only get you so far, and the worldwide pandemic prevented me from being able to travel for specific reconnaissance. So I had to lean on a number of subject matter experts for their help and critical eyes.

Paul Scurfield provided valuable early feedback on some chapters involving saturation diving and Jason Van der Schyff reviewed the book near its completion with the same focus. Their input was essential to getting those scenes as accurate and believable as possible, though I still took some liberties.

My week diving the wreck of HMS *Hermes* back in 2017 informed much of my knowledge of the east coast of Sri Lanka, deep tech diving, and World War II shipwrecks. The Deep Sea Resort in Batticaloa was the inspiration for The Deep Blue in *Depth Charge*. I owe a debt of gratitude to the Deep Sea's owner, Felician Fernando, who inspired my character, Sebastian, and taught me the art of technical diving and introduced me to the *Hermes*.

My time spent with the Lost Ships of Cortés Project in Mexico opened my eyes to the world of underwater archaeology and inspired the character, and the work, of my hero, Tusker. I thank Fritz Hanselmann, Christopher Horrell, Melanie Damour, and Jonathan Kingston for allowing me to get a glimpse into their work.

To understand the nuances of Sri Lankan Buddhism and a history of Buddhist extremism, I turned to my friend, Milinda Cumaratunga. Milo reviewed excerpts of this novel, provided valuable feedback, suggested appropriate names, and corrected my often blundered portrayal of the lives and customs of the Buddhist clergy.

Tina Edward read a draft of *Depth Charge* and provided feedback on some portrayals of Sri Lankan life, and for her time and comments, I am grateful.

To make sure I was getting the titles, clothing, and lingo correct with regard to World War II Britain, as well as some Cambridge and London geography, I asked historian John Henry Phillips to review select chapters, and he gave me helpful feedback and suggestions.

Tom Bushey provided intel on Michigan's Upper Peninsula, specifically the location where Tusker's family cabin is, where he learned to scuba dive.

Years before I even conceived of *Depth Charge*, I read a thriller by Pierre Gobinet called *The Freelancers*. I remember thinking, "This is the kind of novel I want to write." I met Pierre on a cold night in Geneva, where he told me about his experience writing that novel, and I credit him with being a big inspiration to me. If you can find *The Freelancers*, I highly recommend it.

Even as I was writing the first few chapters of *Depth Charge*, Andrew Revitt reached out to provide incredibly kind encouragement and real world advice on publishing and promoting my novel. It was on his suggestion that I set up the *Depth Charge* website and collected contact information from interested readers. Andrew also provided a cover art concept that I used as inspiration on my earliest manuscripts. Never underestimate the value of seeing your title and name on a book cover early on. It makes it feel official.

J.R. Seeger, a prolific writer and creator of the "Mike 4" thriller series, reached out and generously offered advice and encouragement, and sent me one of his novels to read. Now that *Depth Charge* is published, I am returning the favor, sending a copy to J.R., and I hope he enjoys it.

How can I adequately thank Paul Andrews? This hard working London-based designer offered his time and talents free of charge to create not only the book cover design, but all of my marketing images, animations, logos, and even did the typesetting of this book. It was an act of extreme generosity that I'll never forget.

Similarly generous was my friend and talented composer, Oran Chan, who, upon seeing an early cover mockup, took it upon himself to compose an entire theme song for *Depth Charge*. I have never heard of a novel having its own soundtrack, but listening to the track on repeat was inspiring as I edited the book, and it will find its way into the audiobook and, one day, the film score (a writer can dream, right?).

My friend Rick Marei learned that Tusker's diving watch was to be an Aquastar Benthos, and he generously provided me with some inspiration in the form of a vintage Benthos to wear while I wrote *Depth Charge*.

Growing up in suburban Milwaukee wasn't the most exotic or exciting life, but I found a kindred, dreaming spirit in my oldest friend, Christopher Winters. In high school, Chris and I shared musical tastes, wrote poetry, and went to coffeehouses while other friends were partying. Later on, it was with Chris that I did my first shipwreck dive, and we've shared countless adventures both topside and underwater in years hence. The fact is, I always looked up to Chris. He took up acting, wrote a children's book as a teenager, and took a bus to New York to try to get it published. He later became an award-winning maritime historian, author, and photographer. His focus, drive, and talents have always been an inspiration to me. Oh, and on a trip to Sri Lanka together, Chris started calling me "Tusker."

Back when I was writing for *Gear Patrol*, I worked with a young editor named Chris Wright. I sparred with Chris occasionally over his suggested changes to my articles, but deep down I knew he was usually right and he made me a better writer. I told Chris that one day when I wrote my first book, I wanted him to edit it. With *Depth Charge*, that day arrived, and I cannot emphasize enough how much his editing improved the book you are reading. If you're going to write a novel, never, ever, skip the editing. And if you can, hire Chris to edit it.

Nick Milanes, another *Gear Patrol* alum, came recommended by Chris to do the proofreading of the final layout. It takes a certain kind of person to proofread a 60,000-word, 300-page book full of foreign names and arcane diving references, and Nick is that person. There's nothing worse than opening a new novel and finding mistakes and typos, and the fact that *Depth Charge* looks so good is largely down to Nick.

The idea for *Depth Charge* was hatched in Jamaica, fittingly while my wife, Gishani, and I were staying at Goldeneye, Ian Fleming's former estate. We were sitting by the lagoon after a morning snorkel when I got a bit of bad career news over e-mail. The decision to embark on a novel crystallized right there, and we immediately starting hatching plot ideas and possible publishing strategies, mere meters from where all of the James Bond novels were written.

The simple fact is, not only would *Depth Charge* never have been written, but I'd never have become the writer I am, if it weren't for Gishani. Over our two decades together, she has always encouraged, cajoled, scolded, motivated, critiqued, and supported my writing efforts. She was there with me when I was writing my gear and watch reviews, taking the photos. And she always listens when I read out even my most boring work.

Gishani pored over *Depth Charge*, page by page, helping craft plot, relationships, names, and giving honest feedback on readability. She helped set up the *Depth Charge* website and has promised to help package and ship the books when orders come in. And she has supported us both, without complaint, while I spent months chasing a dream. Gishani always told me that she believed I'd be a novelist one day. Well, here I am, and it's largely thanks to her.

Finally, what novelist doesn't thank his parents? We often joke that my wife and my mother compete for the title "Number One Fan," but if longevity counts, then Mom wins. As far back as I can remember she encouraged and celebrated my writing, and my reading. She always has been my champion, cheering for me from the bleachers, no matter what I've done or how well I've done it. The love of a mother knows no bounds and I owe a life of happiness and success to her.

Though Dad likes to pretend he keeps a tight rein on their finances, I know he'd relent if Mom decides to buy 100 copies of *Depth Charge*. Dad has always been the rock, the strong support our family relied on while we had our fun. I can't count how many times he bailed me out or lent practical advice, and a lifetime being his son has given me the strength and confidence to even write this book. He's also afraid of deep water, one trait I'm glad I *didn't* inherit from him.

I want to acknowledge two books I read that provided good background for some themes in *Depth Charge*. *Stalin's Gold*, by Barrie Penrose, explores the salvage of gold from a sunken British warship in the Barents Sea. It is a daring story that could have been a thriller if it wasn't true and it provided ideas and inspiration for *Depth Charge*.

The Hermes Adventure, by Rex Morgan, is a fascinating firsthand account of an expedition to dive the HMS *Hermes* wreck, written by the son of the photographer who was on board *Hermes* when it sank in 1942. The book spans three generations and 40 years, from Australia to Sri Lanka, and has some amazing photos and accounts of the ship's sinking by her surviving crew.

Finally, I want to thank all those who encouraged me from the beginning of this project. Despite a lifetime of travel and adventure, both underwater and topside all over the planet, it was the sitting at home during a pandemic that became my life's greatest adventure. The early and continued interest from those who signed up for email updates and sent me emails and messages with advice and encouragement kept me going when I hit moments of writer's block, plot dead-ends, travel restrictions, and other challenges along the way. I hope the book lives up to your expectations and I thank you for your faith in me.

Jason Heaton
Minneapolis
April, 2021

About the Author

Jason Heaton has a decade-long history of adventure, travel, wristwatch, and gear writing, and his work has appeared in *Outside, Gear Patrol, Men's Journal, Wired, Australian Geographic*, and *Hodinkee*. The *New York Times* once called him "a test pilot for the world's most illustrious undersea timepieces." He is also the co-host of the popular podcast *The Grey NATO*.

A certified technical diver, Heaton has been underwater all over the world, from the Galapagos to New Zealand to the Caribbean, and since 2015, he has been a member of the prestigious Explorers Club. He lives with his wife, Gishani, and their two cats in Minneapolis. *Depth Charge* is his first novel.

DEPTH CHARGE

Made in the USA
Las Vegas, NV
05 July 2021